THE LEGEND OF LEXANDROS

Dallas had always felt responsible for her young sister Jane, so when Jane was expecting a baby by rich, young Paris Stavros, who was then killed in a car crash, it all seemed too much for Dallas. So she was in no position to argue when Paris's father, a millionaire Greek shipowner, announced that both Jane and her baby were his responsibility, and that he intended taking both girls forthwith to his private island of Lexandros as Jane refused to go without her sister.

This Large Print Edition
is published by kind permission of
MILLS & BOON LTD.
London

ANNE MATHER

THE LEGEND OF LEXANDROS

Complete and Unabridged

20085

ULVERSCROFT
Leicester

First published 1969

First Large Print Edition
published November 1978

© Anne Mather 1969

British Library CIP Data

Mather, Anne
 The legend of Lexandros. Large print ed.
 (Ulverscroft large print series : romance)
 I. Title
 823'.9'1F   PR6063.A/

 ISBN 0-7089-0226-X

Published by
F. A. Thorpe (Publishing) Ltd.
Anstey, Leicestershire
Printed in England

Love is
a time of enchantment:
in it all days are fair and all fields
green. Youth is blest by it,
old age made benign: the eyes of love see
roses blooming in December,
and sunshine through rain. Verily
is the time of true-love
a time of enchantment—and
Oh! how eager is woman
to be bewitched!

CHAPTER ONE

DALLAS let herself into the flat, juggling with her key, her handbag, and a pile of exercise books which she had brought home for marking. She allowed the books to cascade on to the table in the minute entrance hall of the flat, and pushing open the lounge door, called:

"Jane! I'm home. Are you in?"

There was no reply, and Dallas glanced at her watch thoughtfully. It was already quarter to six, and as Jane's office closed at five o'clock, that could only mean one thing. Paris' Stavros was bringing her home, and they had made a detour on the way.

Dallas sighed heavily, and removing her sheepskin coat she flung it wearily over an armchair. Then, determinedly straightening her shoulders, she walked through to the kitchen to prepare their evening meal. Chops were sizzling appetisingly under the grill when she heard the door open, and Jane came into the lounge humming cheerfully to herself. Dallas walked to the kitchen door and

1

looked at her sister questioningly. "You're late."

Jane nodded. "Paris brought me home. We called at Joe's."

"I thought so." Dallas nodded, and turned back to attend to the potatoes she was frying. "Are you going out this evening?"

Jane had walked into the bedroom. It was a small flat with only one bedroom which they shared. Now she came to the bedroom door, and called:

"Yes, I am. Why? Have you any objections?" Her tone was sarcastic.

Dallas made a helpless movement. "Only the usual ones," she replied, and waited for the explosion. As usual she was not disappointed.

Jane stormed into the kitchen, "Honestly, Dallas, you infuriate me! This is the third time this week. You simply won't believe that Paris loves me, will you?"

"Frankly . . . no." Dallas applied the opener to a can of peas with some savagery. "I may be foolish and old-fashioned, Jane, but I can't really see the only son of the owner of the worldwide Stavros Ship ping Line falling for a . . . well, for a typist like you. Particularly one who works in his father's London branch office!"

Jane's cheeks were scarlet now. "What were you about to call me? A nonentity, perhaps?"

Dallas shrugged. "Well, it's true, isn't it? I mean, be honest with yourself, Jane, just for once. You're no oil painting, and you haven't a penny to your name. Why should he be interested in you when he can have his pick of practically any girl both here and in his native Greece! He only wants you for kicks, Jane, and the sooner you realise it the better. Once you begin to bore him, it will all be over. I just don't want you to get hurt, that's all."

"You have a funny way of showing it," grunted Jane moodily. "Anyway, I know that all you've said is true, in as much as the facts fit the personalities, but Paris loves me! He's told me so, and I believe him!"

"Oh lord!" Dallas raised her eyes heavenward.

"Well, I know what I'm talking about," Jane averred hotly. "Anyway, how would you know whether he loves me or not? I don't believe you know what love is. After all, Charles is hardly anyone's idea of the perfect lover!"

Dallas controlled her temper with difficulty. "I must know a little more than you do," she replied. "In any case, despite your dislike of Charles, I find his love-making perfectly adequate."

Jane screwed up her nose rudely. "It is possible to deceive yourself into believing anything—"

"My point exactly," Dallas interrupted her.

"—and as you've had no other boy-friends since Charles made the scene your experience is as limited as mine," finished Jane triumphantly.

Dallas sighed. "All right, maybe I don't know any more than you do, but at least my common sense tells me that Paris will never get around to discussing marriage lines and wedding rings with you, at any rate."

"Paris acts a whole lot older than his years," said Jane, examining her fingernails.

"That I can believe," remarked Dallas dryly. "And that's another thing. He's experienced and you're not." She reached for her handbag and lit a cigarette. "In any case, he's only spending six months in the London office, isn't he? When does his term give out? Soon, I imagine, and what then?"

Jane turned away. "He has another eight

weeks yet." She looked at Dallas over her shoulder. "The fact that he is actually learning the business from the bottom up should prove to you that he's not just a playboy."

"At his father's instigation, I've no doubt," replied Dallas, inhaling deeply, savouring the relaxation the cigarette engendered.

"You just won't try to understand," cried Jane angrily. "You're so complacent! So sure you know everything!"

"I'm not sure of anything right now," replied Dallas, frowning.

"You're becoming just like Charles," retorted Jane, in disgust. "You're only twenty-two, but you act at least fifteen years older."

"Don't you dare criticise Charles," exclaimed Dallas. "At least he's a decent, honest man."

Jane flounced away to wash and change, and Dallas sighed again, and began dishing up the meal for which she had no appetite. It was always like this. They argued and argued, and got no further forward. Dallas felt sure that Jane secretly thought she was jealous, whereas in actual fact she would have been glad to see Jane dating a boy with a background similar to their own. It was all very well for Jane to talk, but she was not to know that their father had told Dallas to take care of Jane, to look after her always, for she was too much like their mother, who had run away with another man when Dallas was only ten. Jane, at five, had not known much about it, but Dallas had felt the pain and frustration that enveloped her father, never to leave him entirely.

Her father had been an archaeologist, and had spent many weeks away from his wife and family on "digs". Dallas had always been interested to hear all about it on his return, but her mother had hated the lonely life she was forced to lead, and had eventually found someone who could provide her with all the entertainment she craved. They had seen little of her since the divorce, and now she was living in America, and their only communications were birthday and Christmas greetings.

So Dallas felt doubly responsible for her young sister, and there was no one, apart from Charles, to whom she could turn. And she hesitated turning to him, anyway, because he and Jane had never hit it off and were openly antagonistic towards one another. It was for this reason that Dallas had

6

delayed their wedding for so long, concerned about Jane's reactions to living with Charles.

Charles lived with his mother in Maidenhead. His mother owned a large house there, and as she was a semi-invalid, being permanently confined to a wheel-chair, it had been decided that Dallas and Charles should live with her after their wedding. Dallas got along quite well with Mrs. Jennings, and found this idea acceptable, but Jane was too carefree and careless of other people's feelings to ever get along with the Jennings family for long.

After Jane had left that evening, Dallas went into the bedroom to get changed before Charles arrived. He was coming to spend an evening at the flat. They didn't go out together often; Charles liked television and so long as he could see his favourite programmes he didn't mind staying in. Dallas sometimes wished they could go out more often, but with the memory of her mother's behaviour still strong in her mind, she crushed these thoughts with impatient intolerance.

Now she stripped off the dark brown tweed suit which she had worn for school and glanced half critically at herself in the dressing-table mirror. Did Jane really think she was getting like Charles?

Then she shrugged such thoughts away as being disloyal. After all, teaching a class of eight-year-olds as she did required that she dress with some modicum of severity, for otherwise her youthful appearance would maintain no discipline. Besides, Charles did like her in plain clothes and he liked the french pleat in which she invariably dressed her hair. Both girls had long hair, but whereas Jane's was blonde, Dallas's was a glorious red-gold in colour. Studying her features momentarily, she thought that apart from her eyes, her hair was probably her most attractive feature. And Charles was thirty-seven, after all, and naturally he didn't want everyone to think he was going out with a girl far too young for him, her musing continued.

When her thoughts strayed to other things Jane had said, she felt a little disturbed. Her relationship with Charles had never troubled her before, but was it possible that the reasons she had accepted Charles so readily were mixed up with a longing for security and someone else to turn to?

She determinedly thrust such thoughts aside. She was becoming fanciful, and allowing Jane's behaviour to play upon her thoughts too much. It would not do! It simply would not do!

Shedding her underwear, she walked into the tiny alcove which they called a bathroom, and showered hastily. Then she dressed in a warm, green woollen dress, which had seen better days, and rewound her hair into its knot. She refused to consider her reflection any further. Charles liked her like this, and he was all that mattered.

Charles arrived at eight o'clock, punctual to the minute. He was a man of medium height and build, only slightly veering to plumpness. He had known the girls since they were children, having been friendly with their father, and when their father died quite suddenly he had been responsible for getting them this flat, and dealing with the sale of the house in Earl's Court which had been too big and expensive for them to keep on alone.

He kissed Dallas warmly, and said: "Hello, darling. How are you? You're looking a little peaky this evening."

Dallas shrugged. "Oh, can't you guess, Charles? I've had another row with Jane."

"Over Paris Stavros?"

"What else?"

"Well, I wish you wouldn't, Dallas," said

Charles, rather irritatedly. "After all, she isn't a child, and sooner or later she has got to learn that all the apples on the branch aren't sweet ones."

"Don't be pompous," said Dallas, sighing. "Jane is my responsibility, after all, and I can't just let her ruin her life."

"You're over-dramatising the situation, as usual," retorted Charles, shaking his head. "Paris Stavros is only eighteen, when all's said and done. He's not had time to build up much of a reputation! You'd think he was a lecherous old playboy to hear you talk!"

Dallas had to smile at this, and she lit a cigarette thoughtfully, waiting for Charles's exclamation: "Dallas, must you smoke so much?"

She shook her head. "Why not? I don't smoke all day. I deserve some relaxation, don't I?"

Charles deigned not to answer this, and seating himself in front of the television set, said: "Is there anything exciting on this evening?"

"There's that detective series you enjoy," remarked Dallas, feeling strangely restless. "Charles! Why don't we go to the pictures, for a change?"

Charles glanced round frowning. "We never go out on Thursday evenings," he exclaimed, aggrieved.

"Oh, all right, all right!" Dallas sank down on to the couch beside him. "Have you had a busy day?"

Charles was an accountant with a firm here in the city.

"So-so," he answered absently. "Oh, look, Dallas. The programme is just starting!"

Dallas nodded, and drew deeply on her cigarette. Whether it was the continued arguments with Jane, or whether something inside her was beginning to rebel she didn't know, but quite suddenly she could see their lives going on in the same way for years to come, and it was quite frightening. Was this all it was about? If only Charles wasn't such a stick-in-the-mud. She had always excused him on account of his age, but after all, thirty-seven wasn't so old. Lots of men didn't become so set in their ways at that age. It could only be the influence of his mother, and for the first time she wondered if they were doing the right thing, going to live with her after their marriage. It was all very well, and Dallas knew that old Mrs. Jennings was the kind of person who required someone to live with her, but she could get a companion, and they could buy a new house, in one of the new suburban developments, and then they would really have something worth saving for.

"Charles," she said tentatively, "I don't think living with your mother after we're married is such a good idea after all.'

Charles paid little attention to her. He was engrossed with the television play. Dallas nudged him. "Did you hear what I said?"

"What? Oh no, what was that? Can't it wait until after this is over?"

Dallas stiffened. "No, it can't. I . . . I don't want to live with your mother after we're married."

Charles stared at her, aghast. "What?" he said again. "Why?"

Dallas swallowed hard. "Because you're getting too like her. You're old before your time. Good heavens, Charles, you're only thirty-seven, but you act sometimes twenty years older."

Charles's face was bright red now, and Dallas felt awful. But it had to be said.

"Dallas, have you taken leave of your senses?" He stared at her. "The house at Maidenhead is far too big for just Mother

12

alone. Besides, it would be a waste of money buying another house."

Dallas stubbed out her cigarette. "Why? Because you can't afford it?"

Charles twisted his hands together. "I can afford another house, Dallas. But I have no intention of wasting money for no reason."

Dallas shrugged. "All right, then. What if I tell you that those are my conditions for our marriage?"

Charles's mouth dropped open, and then he hastily closed it. "You can't be serious, Dallas. Have you been drinking by any chance?" he asked suspiciously. "This isn't at all like you."

"How do you know what I'm like? You never bother to find out. You merely sit staring at my television all evening, then eat your supper and go."

"Dallas!"

"Well, it's true. I must have been sitting with my eyes closed before, but they're open now. It's no good, Charles. We're young. We deserve a bit of freedom, of time to be alone together, and if we're living with your mother she'll always be around, wanting you to help her into bed, or into the bath, or into her clothes! It's no good. We need a home of our

13

own. I'm quite willing to continue working until such time as we have everything we need."

"After our marriage, you will not work," said Charles firmly. "I wouldn't dream of it." His tone changed. "Dallas, darling Dallas, be reasonable. The house at Maidenhead is so *big*. If you like we needn't even live with Mother. We could have the house equally divided into two flats."

Dallas hesitated. "I don't know," she began, wondering whether she was being unreasonable, and all because of Jane!

"Think about it, then," said Charles, looking hopefully at her. "It would break Mother's heart if she thought she was causing trouble between us."

Dallas wondered if this were true. Mrs. Jennings was too closely involved with her son to allow him to leave her very easily.

"All right," she said now, and Charles leaned forward and switched off the television, looking round gently at her.

"Come here," he said softly, drawing her towards him, and she allowed him to pull her into his arms and put his soft mouth against hers.

★   ★   ★

Much later in the evening Dallas was worried again, and she could tell from Charles's expression that she was annoying him.

"For goodness' sake, Dallas," he said. "It's eleven-fifteen, that's all. Jane will be home very shortly!"

"But, Charles," she began awkwardly, "can't you try and understand? Paris Stavros isn't the kind of boy to be content with dating Jane for nothing. Everyone can see he only dates her for kicks. What if she allows him to . . . well . . ."

Charles lifted his jacket from the back of the couch, and shook his head. "If Jane gets herself into trouble, she'll have to get herself out of it," he replied coldly.

Dallas stared at him disbelievingly. "Don't be so callous," she cried. "Jane is only a baby!"

"Well, don't expect me to mother her when she comes to live with us," remarked Charles. "She'll soon be shown the door if she misbehaves in Maidenhead. There are too many people there who know me——"

"What!" Dallas put her hands on her hips. "What have you got to do with it? Surely you're not going to tell me that your reputation stands in any danger of being smirched!"

"Don't get het-up." Charles decided to take a different line. "All right, Dallas, all right. I'll have a word with her when she comes."

"No, don't do that," exclaimed Dallas, shaking her head. "You're only likely to antagonise her into further trouble. I can deal with her, or at least, I'll try."

Charles put an arm around her shoulders. "I'm sorry if I seem unfeeling, but you seem to have all the responsibilities and it's not fair."

"I'm the eldest," Dallas answered.

Charles was buttoning his overcoat against the cold night air when Jane breezed into the flat, shedding her suede coat and knee-length boots in the hallway.

"Hello, you two," she called. She usually attempted to be friendly towards Charles, Dallas had to concede.

Charles thrust his hands deeply into his overcoat pockets.

"Do you know you've had your sister half out of her mind with worry?" he asked, in a low angry voice.

Jane rubbed her nose and looked at Dallas. "Oh, really? I'm sorry, Dallas. You know how time flies when you're having a good time!"

Charles grunted, and Dallas said: "Charles!" warningly, but he went on: "No, we don't. We've been waiting for your arrival since ten-thirty. I presume that's a reasonable time to expect a seventeen-year-old home."

Jane shrugged, her face flushed. "Can't Dallas catechise me herself?" she asked cheekily, resenting his tone.

Charles stiffened. "Now you listen to me, young woman," he began, but Dallas shook her head.

"Now Charles, please. I can handle this."

"Obviously you can't, or she wouldn't talk to you like that," said Charles angrily. "You'd better change your ways, Jane, before Dallas and I are married, or you may find yourself without a roof over your head!"

Jane stared at him angrily. "All right. I'm quite capable of taking care of myself. I'll keep the flat on. Get someone to share it with me."

Dallas inwardly groaned at the worsening situation, breaking up the argument before it came to blows.

"Go on, Charles," she said, "I've told you, I can handle this."

20085

Charles turned and marched out of the room, followed rather more slowly by Dallas. She hardly noticed the kiss he gave her, so intent was she upon returning to the lounge to have it out again with Jane.

But when she returned, Jane was in the bedroom undressing, and she said, before Dallas could speak:

"Oh, don't start again. I know, I know what you're going to say. But it's no good. I won't give him up."

Dallas shrugged. "All right."

Jane looked strangely at her. "What am I supposed to glean from that remark?"

"Exactly what you like." Dallas stretched wearily. "I'm sick of this whole business. Where did you go this evening, just out of interest?"

"To a club run by a friend of Paris's—a Greek. We danced a lot, and had a few cokes. It was a good evening."

"Do you drink alcohol?" Dallas's question was soft and undemanding, despite its pointedness.

Jane flushed. "No, of course not. I'm under age."

"Would that stop you?"

"Oh, Dallas, stop it! I'm tired."

18

"You have a nerve!" Dallas turned away. "Anyway, why don't you bring him here sometimes? If I met him myself, maybe I wouldn't feel so concerned."

"Paris, here?" Jane laughed. "I couldn't do that."

"Why not?"

"Well . . . I mean . . . his apartment is huge, with gorgeous furniture . . ."

"You've been to his apartment? When? I thought you always went to clubs?"

Jane grimaced. "Heavens, what have I said! Why shouldn't I go to his apartment?"

Dallas unloosened her hair from its knot and it fell in a cascade of colour about her shoulders. Caught off guard, Jane said:

"Why don't you always wear your hair loose? You look so much younger! You make me feel so mean, Dallas, because I know you're only a little older than I am, and you're having a hell of a time with me, aren't you?" She half smiled. "It's only when you look so schoolmarmish, and Charles is there beside you like a bloodhound, that I forget who you really are. Dallas, please try and understand."

"It's no good, Jane," said Dallas wearily. "We stand at opposite sides of the line. You can't see what's under your nose, and I can't believe he's sincere!"

Jane hunched her shoulders. "Well, there's nothing you, or Charles, can do. I love Paris, and I intend to go on seeing him." She tugged angrily at her hair with a comb. "Whatever you say!"

★　★　★

A week later Dallas had made a decision, brought about mainly by the fact that Jane was no longer telling her the truth. Her breath had smelled strongly of alcohol two evenings when she came home, and Dallas, who had been in bed pretending to be asleep, had lain awake for hours after Jane's breathing had become smooth and regular. Jane was also beginning to look drawn and tired, for late nights combined with early mornings were making their presence felt. Dallas seemed continually in a state of anxiety, and she wished wholeheartedly that Paris Stavros would find himself another girl-friend soon.

Unable to expect any useful assistance or advice from Charles, Dallas decided her only course of action was to try and contact

Alexander Stavros, the boy's father. It seemed a vain hope; Alexander Stavros lived in Greece, and she had no earthly idea how she could reach him there.

Besides, even if she could contact him, why should he care what happened to her sister, so long as Paris was happy? Unless the threat of a scandal might deter him. Maybe he was a man with a heart; maybe she could appeal to his better judgement.

Dallas felt desperate. She was clutching at straws and she knew it. And then, as though fate was lending her a helping hand, she read one morning, in her newspaper going to work, that Alexander Stavros had arrived in England the previous day to visit his son, and to have trade talks with British businessmen. A casual word about it to Jane that evening brought forth a veritable stream of information about him, gleaned no doubt from Paris himself, and within a short time Dallas knew that he was staying at the Dorchester, and would be there for approximately a fortnight.

Deciding not to mention her decision to Charles, Dallas telephoned the Dorchester the following morning and asked to speak to Mr. Stavros. A polite receptionist advised her that Mr. Stavros was not in the hotel, but if she wished she might speak to one of his secretaries.

"*One* of his secretaries!" exclaimed Dallas, in astonishment, and then, swallowing hard, she said: "When will Mr. Stavros be back?"

"I really couldn't say," replied the receptionist smoothly. "Excuse me, but who shall I say has called?"

"I . . . I . . . he won't know me," began Dallas awkwardly, and would have said more, but the receptionist interrupted her.

"I would suggest you speak to one of the secretaries," she said, in a cool tone. "Mr. Stavros doesn't take calls in the normal way. I'm sure Mr. Saravanos would be able to help you."

Dallas hesitated for a moment. "But this is a personal matter," she said, running her tongue over suddenly dry lips. "Is there no way I can contact Mr. Stavros direct?"

"Excuse me, but I have other calls to attend to," said the receptionist, avoiding a direct answer.

"Very well." Dallas was forced to ring off. She came out of the telephone kiosk dejectedly. It was mid-morning break at the school, and she had slipped across the road to make her call. There seemed no alternative but to ring again tomorrow and speak to one of the secretaries.

The next day she could not concentrate on her work. She put off making the call to the Dorchester all day, hating the way she was having to put herself into such an awkward position. What would Alexander Stavros think of her when she did get to see him, or should she say "if"? It was doubtful indeed whether a man in his position would bother about a nobody like herself.

She went home after work, made the evening meal for Jane and herself, and then waited until Jane had dressed for a date with Paris and gone out before thinking seriously about ringing the hotel again. To humble herself in this way was alien to her nature and the thought of asking him now to stop his son from meeting Jane seemed stupid and childish.

She felt sure she would never have the nerve to go through with it, no matter what the consequences to Jane might be. It could only look bad. She would seem like the ugly sister trying to keep Cinderella from the ball.

She smiled at her thoughts, and then hunched her shoulders. It was all very well deciding in the heat of the moment to see

Alexander Stavros, but now, in cold blood, it was fast becoming untenable.

She washed the dishes, wiped down the draining board, and eventually put the dishes back into the cupboard. Then she walked into the lounge.

The television was playing to itself, so she switched it off and walked into the bedroom. She sat in front of the dressing-table mirror studying her reflection for a few minutes, trying not to think of the task ahead of her.

Then she pulled open the dressing-table drawer to take out a handkerchief when something else, caught on the lace of the handkerchief, fell with a thud on the carpet. Bending, she picked it up. It was a bracelet, but such a bracelet as Dallas had never seen before. It was, or looked like, solid gold, with inlaid stones of red and blue which looked like rubies and sapphires. Dallas dropped it hastily back in the drawer, as though it burned her. She had no doubts as to its origin; Paris must have given it to Jane, but why?

Any doubts left in her mind as to the advisability of her task fled away. She had no choice but to try and do something before it was too late.

She changed into navy blue stretch pants and a scarlet anorak of Jane's. It was a cold evening and such attire was more suitable than the short skirts she usually wore. But she smiled to herself when she thought of Charles's displeasure if he could see her now. He hated casual clothes, and preferred Dallas to wear tailored suits and dresses, with little adornment. Her hair had come loose from its immaculate pleat, so instead of putting it up again, she combed it out, leaving it loose about her shoulders. She touched a coral lipstick to her mouth, and then ran down the steps out of the block of flats. The telephone kiosk was a couple of blocks away and Jane was often saying they should have one of their own, but Dallas could see no point when in a little over four months they would be living in Charles's semi-detached house at Maidenhead which already had a phone.

Charles was not coming up to town this evening and Dallas felt a carefree liveliness assail her as she walked to the telephone. Sometimes Charles was a little too over-bearing.

The kiosk was already occupied, so she stood around stamping her feet to stop the chilling wind from piercing the warm quilted lining of the anorak, and then when the man emerged, she slid inside thankfully. It was March, but so cold it could have been January, and spring seemed a long way away.

Dallas rang the Dorchester, and inserted her money, and when the receptionist answered, a man this time, she felt relieved. At least she would not have the ignominy of asking the same questions to the same girl.

But when she asked for Mr. Stavros, the man's answers were practically the same as the girl's had been. So deciding she might as well speak to the secretary, a Mr. Karantinos, she was put through to the suite.

A maid answered at first, and then she heard the accented tones of Stephanos Karantinos.

"Oh . . . er . . . good evening," said Dallas, biting hard on her lip. "Would it be possible for me to speak to Mr. Stavros? It's a personal matter."

"Mr. Stavros is changing for an evening engagement," replied Stephanos Karantinos. "Surely I can be of assistance. You say it is of a personal nature. In what way is this so?" He was polite, but unyielding.

Dallas sighed. "It's to do with Paris, Mr. Stavros's son. He is at present going around with my sister Jane."

"Yes?" The voice was clipped. "This is what you wish to speak to Mr. Stavros about?"

"Yes. I . . . I . . . want it stopped!"

She was aware she had shocked the man, but in an amused way, for he burst out laughing, and she felt unreasonably angry.

"It's no laughing matter," she exclaimed hotly, and then heard the sound of voices as though someone else had joined him and was asking what the joke might be. There was more laughter, and then another voice reached her ears, a deep attractive voice, with barely a trace of accent.

"Alexander Stavros speaking. To whom do I address myself?" His tone was mocking, but Dallas was too relieved to be actually speaking to Stavros himself to care.

"My name is Dallas Collins, Mr. Stavros," she answered shakily. "This . . . this is rather difficult for me, but my sister Jane works for your company in the London office, and she is at present infatuated with your son Paris. I want you, if you will, to use your influence to stop this affair before anything unfortunate happens."

"Unfortunate? For whom?"

"For Jane, of course."

"Indeed?" There was a silence for a moment, and then he continued: "It seems to me, Miss Collins, that you are interfering in something which is actually no concern of yours."

"No concern? Jane is only seventeen. Our parents are dead, and I am her guardian!"

"Paris is only eighteen, Miss Collins."

Dallas sighed heavily. "I know that. Look, Mr. Stavros, I can quite see that this might sound rather ridiculous, but if you knew the circumstances . . ." Her voice trailed away.

"Calm yourself, Miss Collins. Things are never as bad as they seem." She could tell from his tone that he was not so amused now. "I am not satisfied that Paris could do your sister any harm, Miss Collins. He is an intelligent boy, not a moron!" He seemed to be thinking for a few moments, and then he said: "I do not care to discuss my private affairs over the telephone. I have a dinner engagement, but I will cancel it. I suggest you come here to see me, Miss Collins, so that we may discuss this matter more fully."

"Oh, but . . ." Dallas swallowed hard. "I . . . I couldn't do that!"

"Why not? This is not a clandestine meeting, Miss Collins. My secretary,

28

Stephanos, will be present. No matter what you may think of my son, I can assure you I have no interest in you personally."

His tone was arrogant and assured, and Dallas felt like banging the phone down and forgetting she had ever rung him. But she couldn't do that so she said with ill grace: "All right, Mr. Stavros. But I can't think of anything more to say."

Alexander Stavros merely said: "I'll expect you in fifteen minutes, yes? Or is that not long enough?"

"I . . . I'll do my best." Dallas rang off, and came out of the kiosk frowning deeply. Now what had she let herself in for?

A bus deposited her near the Dorchester hotel, and she approached its entrance with some trepidation. She wished she had had time to go home and change before this meeting, but Stavros's arrogant command to be at the hotel in fifteen minutes had left no room for anything, although she was supremely conscious of the shortcomings of pants and an anorak as attire for an evening in the West End of London. Still, she argued with herself, she had no desire to impress the man. If he took a dislike to her, he might wish more readily to resolve the relationship between his son and her sister.

She approached the reception desk cautiously, aware of the curious eyes turned in her direction, and expecting every moment to be brought up short by the sound of an arresting voice. But nothing happened, and the receptionist himself had obviously been forewarned of her arrival because he treated her with respect, and asked her politely to wait while he rang the Stavros suite.

In a few minutes which actually seemed like aeons to Dallas, she was approached by a small, slim dark man with greying hair, and a kind and good-natured appearance. Dallas rose hastily to her feet. Was this Alexander Stavros, then? Heavens, she thought, at least he looks understanding, even though his appearance did not quite line up with her picture of him after hearing that arrogant voice over the phone.

But her expectations were doomed from the start. "Good evening, Miss Collins," he said, smiling. "My name is Stephanos Karantinos. I am secretary to Mr. Stavros."

His secretary! Dallas sighed, and said: "I'm Dallas Collins, how do you do?"

"Come," he said, taking her arm. "Mr. Stavros is waiting to see you."

A lift transported them to the upper regions of the hotel, and Stephanos Karantinos looked rather strangely at Dallas.

"Tell me, Miss Collins," he said, leaning against the wall of the lift as it glided silently upwards, "is your sister like you?"

Dallas shrugged. "I . . . I . . . well . ... in some ways."

Stephanos Karantinos slid his hands into the pockets of his trousers. "Paris has good taste," he remarked, as casually as though they were discussing the weather, and Dallas turned bright red with embarrassment.

She was relieved when the lift halted and Stephanos straightened, and indicated she should precede him along the pile-carpeted corridor that confronted them. She was a mass of nerves and she hardly knew what to expect.

Double white doors admitted them to the suite of rooms taken over by the Stavros company, and Dallas paused on the cream-coloured pile carpet just inside the suite doors felling hopelessly out of her depth. Stephanos Karantinos closed the doors, and crossed the short space which gave on to two shallow steps which separated the rest of this huge lounge from the entrance.

Dallas stared about her in astonishment. She had never, not even with her father, experienced such luxury—white leather chairs and scarlet drapes, Swedish wood and lots of low divans covered in rugs. She stood there in her pants and anorak feeling like the cat who went to look at the queen.

And as though to deepen this image a woman rose lazily from one of the divans at their entrance and stared across at Dallas mockingly, scarlet-tipped nails vivid against the black cigarette holder she was using.

Dallas's eyes were drawn to her as she was the only other occupant of the room, and she wondered who the woman was. Her hair, very dark and sleek, was swept into a high knot on the top of her head, and the pure white silk sheath she was wearing clung lovingly to every line of her body, leaving little to the imagination. Dallas supposed she was beautiful, but there was something repulsive about the slanted eyes, and small, yet perfect, mouth.

Stephanos Karantinos turned at the foot of the steps, and said:

"Come in, Miss Collins, and sit down." He indicated a low chair, and Dallas walked slowly forward and did as he asked. "Mr.

Stavros will not be long. Will you have a drink? A cocktail, perhaps?"

Dallas shook her head. "I don't think so, thank you."

"Oh, come on. Something, at least." Stephanos grinned. "I will mix you a long light drink myself. Something you will enjoy, I can assure you."

Dallas half smiled, trying to relax, while the other woman looked on smilingly. "Stephanos can be very persuasive," she said. "But not always polite. He hasn't introduced us, so let me introduce myself. I'm Athene Siametrou."

Dallas managed a faint greeting, while Stephanos Karantinos mixed her drink, and then handed her a long glass.

"Athene needs no introduction," he remarked dryly. "She can be relied upon not to let herself be overlooked." His tone was light, but with an undertone of sarcasm, and Dallas wondered why.

To her surprise and relief, however, the drink was delicious—a mixture of lime and lemon and Advocaat, and something else which she couldn't quite put a name to, it was very warming, and she sipped it gratefully.

She was accepting a cigarette from a box

which Stephanos Karantinos had offered her when a door to one side of the apartment opened, and she glanced up nervously to see a man entering the room. For a brief moment their eyes met, and then Dallas looked sharply away, trying to concentrate on lighting her cigarette. But in that split second she had registered everything about him and she wondered why she suddenly felt an intense feeling of dismay. He was certainly nothing like she had imagined, her idea being confused with vague pictures of successful businessmen sporting balding heads and overweight bodies, and unfeelingly predatory features.

Alexander Stavros was none of these things. He was tall, and lean, and wore his clothes immaculately. He was intensely dark; dark-haired, dark-skinned, and dark-eyed, and although Dallas knew he must be forty or more, he certainly did not look it. She could imagine that he attracted women like a magnet; he presented so much of a challenge, for as well as his obvious physical attraction, he was wealthy, and she wondered whether his wife found it difficult to retain his interest when she had so much competition. Her own reactions were difficult to assimilate. She was so conscious of the insignificance of her own position, and she could not help but wonder what his relations were with Athene Siametrou, and whether a man like this could possibly care about the moral obligations of his son.

He took out a slim platinum case, extracted a cheroot, and placing it between his teeth he lit it before speaking. Then he walked lazily across the room to where Dallas was sitting, feeling as though her knees were about to start knocking together. His eyes were appraising and she felt apprehensive.

Athene Siametrou rose to her feet again. She had subsided on to the divan earlier, but with Alexander Stavros's entrance she became animated once more. With a husky, entreating tone in her voice she said something swiftly in Greek, or so Dallas surmised, and gazed up into Alexander Stavros's eyes.

Stavros shook his head abruptly, and said: "Speak English, Athene. Our visitor cannot understand you." His expression was sardonic. "But I understand you very well, and you understand me, and therefore there will be no more talk of our engagement this evening. Yes?" He looked down at Dallas thoughtfully, before continuing: "I had thought I mentioned that you should go. Why are you still here?"

Dallas shivered. She thought that if ever he spoke to her like that, in that cold, almost hateful voice, she would curl up inside. But Athene merely sighed herself, and said:

"You are a *pig*, darling." She looked down at Dallas condescendingly. "Take it easy, Miss Collins. You are dealing with complete ruthlessness . . . on occasion. On other occasions he can be quite . . . *charming*." She laughed, and swept up the steps to the entrance where she lifted a dark-brown fur, and slung it carelessly about her shoulders. "Goodbye, darling! See you soon!"

She went out, closing the door with a flourish, and causing a mild chuckle from Stephanos Karantinos's direction.

Dallas sipped her drink, avoiding Alexander Stavros's eyes as he seated himself opposite her, legs apart, his hands hanging loosely between.

"Now," he said, his eyes intent. "You are Miss Collins."

Dallas looked up. "Yes, I'm Dallas Collins."

Alexander Stavros nodded, and then

glanced across at Stephanos. "Get me a drink!" he said. "You know what."

Stephanos straightened up from his lounging position near the window and walked across to the cocktail cabinet which occupied one corner of the room.

"And what is your objection to your sister going out with my son?" Stavros asked, drawing on his cheroot.

Dallas stubbed out her cigarette in a nearby ashtray, playing for time. Now that it had come to the point she felt bereft of reasons.

"I . . . well . . . Jane is an impressionable child. Paris's attentions are destroying all her girlish ways. She has become avaricious and discontented."

"Oh, come now!" Stavros's face mirrored his amusement. "You can't possibly blame this on my son!"

"But I do!" Dallas's confidence returned at his attitude. "Jane was quite contented to live the kind of life she has always lived until she started dating your son. Naturally, he moves in a different circle from her, the girls have more clothes, more money, they can do as they like, they don't have jobs to do all day like Jane."

Alexander Stavros shrugged his broad

shoulders. "Surely your sister is quite capable of seeing these things for herself."

"Jane takes Paris seriously! She really believes that people from different walks of life, different backgrounds, can meet on equal terms if they love one another!"

"And I take it you do not." Stavros's tone was derisive.

Dallas flushed. "Do you?"

Stavros rose to his feet before replying. When he did he ignored her question. "Tell me, Miss Collins, have you ever been in love?"

"I . . . of course!"

"So it is not a question of jealousy, so far as your sister is concerned?"

"*Jealousy?*" Dallas stood up now. "How dare you?"

Stephanos Karantinos handed Stavros his drink, and at his employer's nod left the room.

Dallas walked to the steps, standing down her half-empty glass.

"It seems I'm wasting my time," she said, coldly, fortified by her own anger at his words. "Goodbye, Mr. Stavros!"

"Wait!" Stavros swallowed half his drink, and turned away. "It was only a thought, one

which I didn't place any faith in, anyway."
He seemed preoccupied for a moment. "Have
you asked your sister to stop meeting Paris?"

"Of course."

"And she refuses?"

"Yes."

Stavros shook his head. "And what do you
expect me to do?"

"Well, obviously, you are his father. Your
control over him must be practically
absolute."

"Not necessarily, although I will admit that
I control his income, and without his income
Paris is less . . . shall we say . . . effective."
He smiled, rather sardonically, Dallas
thought. "It is certainly an original experience for me to meet someone with
apparently such little regard for money. Most
of my acquaintances judge everything by the
price for which it can be bought. This applies
to people as well as things. A less, shall I say,
conscientious person than yourself might see
in this situation a chance to inveigle money
out of it."

Dallas stiffened. "As you say, I am not that
kind of person!"

Stavros walked lazily across to the apartment windows, and looked down on the

fairyland of lights that was London spread out below him.

"Don't be so quick to sense offence, Miss Collins," he said dryly. "You created this situation, I did not." He leaned back against the window frame. "Tell me about your background. What do you do?"

Dallas's cheeks burned again. "What I do is not important."

"No, but I am interested."

Dallas sighed. "Well, I'm a teacher."

"Is that so?" His expression resumed its amused appearance. "You do not look like any schoolteacher of my acquaintance."

"Appearances can be deceptive," said Dallas shortly.

"Yes, I'll accept that. And is that your whole ambition? To be a teacher, I mean."

Dallas resented this questioning, but could see no way to avoid it if she wanted Alexander Stavros to use his influence on her behalf. She felt certain he was aware of this, too, and was merely amusing himself by seeing how far she was prepared to go to answer his queries.

Now she said: "Naturally, I want to get married. Have a family."

"So? And there is a man in your scheme of

40

things, who you have met already, who will provide these things for you?'' The sarcasm was evident in his voice. "One, of course, who is from your own small sphere!''

"As a matter of fact, yes," retorted Dallas coldly. "I am engaged to be married."

"I see. And your sister, what will she do when you get married?"

"She will live with Charles and myself, naturally."

"And does she want to?"

Dallas was tired. "Whether she wants to or not is not important. We can give her a home, and security, and that's all she needs."

The room echoed with the sound of his laughter. "My dear Miss Collins," he exclaimed, sobering, "you can't be serious! Do you honestly believe that so long as a person is fed and watered, and given a place to sleep, life goes on its natural course?"

"No . . . that is . . ." Dallas bent her head. "You're deliberately misunderstanding me, Mr. Stavros. Jane was perfectly happy before she met Paris. Once his influence is lifted, she will be happy again."

"And you, Miss Collins, are too naïve to be true!" His tone was harsh and angry now. "There are people who live ecstatically happy

41

lives and yet, by so doing, do not conform to any of your petty little rules! Just because you are prepared to accept less than complete contentment, do not expect everyone to be the same." He stubbed out his cheroot savagely, and Dallas felt her spirits sink to their lowest ebb. If she had really angered him, then her hopes that he might help her were doomed from the outset.

She climbed the shallow steps and walked to the door slowly. When she reached the door, she turned and looked back. Alexander Stavros was standing moodily in the centre of the room, his hands thrust deep into his pockets, his dark eyes brooding. Dallas felt a strange feeling in the pit of her stomach as she looked at him, and she found herself wondering again what his wife was like. For the first time in her life she found herself confronted by a situation she couldn't control. She had always considered herself sane and sensible, and certainly not the type of person to ever be attracted to a man like this, and yet Stavros could not help his attraction, any more than she, as a woman, could help being aware of it, and she thought it was as well that she would never meet him again. Perhaps Jane's involvement with Paris Stavros fitted into the same category. And as Paris had shown an immediate interest in Jane, her sister could not help but feel flattered.

"So," he said slowly, " you are leaving, Miss Collins. I have . . . enjoyed our little conversation. It has been quite enlightening, believe me!"

Dallas did not reply. There seemed nothing more to be said. She merely opened the door, and closing it felt a feeling of depression sweep over her.

CHAPTER TWO

AT the weekend Dallas was astonished to find that Jane was not seeing Paris. After her conversation with Alexander Stavros, Dallas had thought that her intervention could only have had an adverse effect on the whole affair, and she could hardly believe that he had actually spoken to Paris. But whatever he had said, it was obvious that Jane knew nothing about her actions, and for this she was grateful.

Charles arrived on Saturday afternoon to take her down to Maidenhead for the rest of the day, and Dallas impulsively suggested that Jane might go with them.

But Jane was not so keen, and merely declined politely in favour of staying at home and washing her hair. Dallas left her with some misgivings. If Paris had finished with her, she would be better with company than moping at home alone. However, there was nothing she could say, so she had to agree and go with Charles reluctantly.

Mrs. Jennings was waiting for them

impatiently, and Dallas was forced to spend the afternoon talking to her while Charles went out to do some gardening. Mrs. Jennings was not the best of conversationalists, and consequently Dallas was prodded into doing most of the talking. It was apparent that Charles had been unable to contain the information about Dallas wanting them to have a home of their own, for the first thing Mrs. Jennings said was:

"Charles tells me that he is thinking of converting this house into two flats."

Dallas felt her cheeks burn. "Oh, is he?" she temporised.

"You know he is. It was your suggestion, wasn't it?"

"No, not exactly. I thought we ought to have a place of our own."

"Stuff and nonsense," said Mrs. Jennings rudely. "Charles and I get along very well together. I wouldn't care to have anyone else about the place."

"But I'm going to be about the place," replied Dallas firmly. "And Charles is going to be *my* husband. I think I ought to have some say in the matter."

Mrs. Jennings looked annoyed. "All these new-fangled ideas! When I was a young girl, I would have been delighted to have a roof over my head, let alone anything else. A big house like this, going to waste!"

"I know, I know, but naturally I want to buy the things we will use; our furniture, our curtains, our own home!"

"You're an ungrateful girl," exclaimed Mrs. Jennings. "I expect it's that flighty young sister of yours putting ideas into your head!"

"Let's leave Jane out of this," began Dallas hotly.

"Why? She has to do with it, hasn't she? Running around with that Stavros boy! Well, she needn't think she'll get away with that kind of behaviour once she's living here!"

It was quite one thing for Dallas to find fault with Jane, but quite another for a comparative stranger like Mrs. Jennings, and Dallas felt her blood boiling at her prudish remarks.

"I doubt whether Jane will want to live here," she said, controlling her temper with difficulty. "In any case, the wedding is still four months away. There's plenty of time for more discussions nearer the date."

Mrs. Jennings grunted, but was forced to change the subject when Dallas refused to say any more. But Dallas herself felt a rising sense of frustration. Were she and Charles always going to have to adhere to rules made by his mother? And did Charles want things differently, anyway?

In the week that followed Dallas was tempted many times to question Jane as to the reason for her not meeting Paris, but she knew she could not do this. She had to wait until Jane was ready to tell her herself. The only time Jane did go out was to the cinema with a girl-friend, and she was home soon after ten as expected.

Dallas was relieved, and yet she could not believe it could be as easy as all that. Jane had been too adamant before to give Paris up without a fight, and Paris himself, from what she had heard, did not sound like the kind of boy to be intimidated by threats.

She was concerned, too, about Jane, in another way. Her sister did not look well, and her appetite was practically non-existent. At first Dallas had put it down to the enforced separation from Paris, but after a while she began to wonder whether that was all it was. Jane looked so tired in the mornings, and seemed to have lost the vitality she had possessed in such abundance.

Dallas was worried, and could not hide her feelings entirely from Charles, but when he managed to gain her confidence sufficiently to be told the reasons for her concern, he scoffed at her.

"Heavens, Dallas, what do you want? A couple of weeks ago you were worried because she was going out with Paris Stavros. Now you're worried because she's not! You don't make sense!"

"I know, I know. It's just . . . oh, Charles, I have a premonition. Things aren't as simple as you'd have me believe."

"Rubbish! The child has been brought to her senses, that's all. Your talks to her must have borne fruit. I must confess I was surprised at first, but now I can accept it, why can't you?"

Dallas flushed. She had told no one of her visit to Alexander Stavros, not even Charles, for she feared his anger about her intervention.

"I don't know," she said, now. "Maybe it just seems too good to be true!"

The following weekend Dallas was awakened early on Sunday morning by a loud knocking on the door of the flat. Drowsy with sleep, she slid out of bed and as she did so she saw that Jane's bed was empty. She frowned. That was strange. Jane never rose first on a Sunday morning.

Pulling on a turquoise quilted housecoat, she brushed back the tumbled cloud of her hair and walked through the lounge to the front door, trying as she did so to register the events of the previous evening.

She had gone to Maidenhead with Charles as usual, and when she came home Jane was in bed again, as she had been the previous week. She had thought nothing of it and respecting Jane's silence assumed she was asleep. So where was she now? Had she got up early and gone out and forgotten her key?

She pulled open the door and blinked at the man who stood on the threshold. He was tall and dark, like Alexander Stavros, she thought unwillingly, but there the resemblance ended. This man had a black moustache and beard, and was typically Greek in appearance. He was dressed in a thick fur-lined coat, and looked broad and muscular.

Dallas shivered involuntarily. "Yes? What do you want?"

"You are Miss Dallas Collins?"

"Yes."

"Good. Will you get dressed and come

49

with me, please. Mr. Stavros wishes to see you. Mr. Alexander Stavros!"

Dallas swallowed hard. "I . . . I don't understand. Why should Mr. Stavros want to see me?"

"That is for him to tell you," replied the man solemnly. "I will wait."

"Now look here," began Dallas hotly. "I want to know what all this is about. You can't expect me to walk out of here with you without any kind of explanation whatsoever."

The man half smiled. "Mr. Stavros thought you might say that. Very well. I am Myron Saravanos, secretary to Mr. Stavros. He wishes to speak to you concerning your sister and his son Paris. They ran away together last night."

"What!" Dallas was horrified.

"You have not missed your sister?"

"No. At least . . . not until just now. I saw she wasn't in bed." Dallas felt near to tears suddenly. "Oh, please come in. I must get dressed. Does Mr. Stavros know where they've gone?"

"He will explain," said Myron Saravanos calmly. "Do not be alarmed. They will be found and brought home. It is unfortunate, but not irrevocable."

"You're so . . . so . . . detached!" Dallas closed the door as he entered the room, and then hurried into the bedroom to dress.

She did not stop to think what she was putting on, and found herself wearing the green tweed dress which she had worn the previous evening and her sheepskin jacket.

"I'm ready," she said, after she had hastily run a comb through her long hair. "Shall we go?"

A low red limousine awaited them outside, chauffeur-driven and luxurious, but Dallas had no thought to give to her surroundings. Her mind was in a turmoil, her tired brain alive with the knowledge that she had been right all along. It had been out of character for Jane to submit so easily. But what now?

Alexander Stavros was waiting in the suite of the hotel. Dressed in close-fitting dark blue pants and a navy blue knitted shirt, he looked restless and arrogant, pacing about the cream-carpeted floor. He stopped at their entrance and said:

"So, Miss Collins, it seems your fears were justified."

Dallas nodded, not trusting herself to speak, and without asking her whether she wanted a drink or not he poured out a

51

generous measure of brandy, added a little water, and said:

"Drink that. It will restore your confidence as well as your voice."

Dallas took the drink, accepted a cigarette, and sank down into a low armchair.

"Wh . . . where have they gone?" she asked, after she had taken a few sips of the spirit and felt it burning its way into her stomach.

"Of that I am not certain," he said, shrugging. "Knowing Paris, I doubt whether he is positive himself of his destination."

"But . . . I mean . . . don't you think they may be making for Scotland?"

"For Scotland?" He stared at her. "Ah, yes, you mean Gretna Green, yes?" and at her nod, his face assumed a strange expression. "I confess I doubt whether my son has marriage in mind," he said harshly.

Dallas's cheeks paled, and he gave an ejaculation. "Oh, really, Miss Collins, don't pass out on me. Surely even you are not so old-fashioned as to imagine that every couple who run away make for Gretna Green!"

"No, but how can you be so sure?"

He shrugged. "My son and I had a short conversation on the subject of English girls," he said. "Paris told me then that he had no intention of becoming seriously involved with anyone here. He is perfectly aware of his obligations to me and to his fiancée in Lexandros."

"His *fiancée*?" echoed Dallas weakly.

"I am afraid so. His marriage has been arranged for many years, and his fiancée is the daughter of one of my greatest friends. You see, Miss Collins, in Greece we are still a little old-fashioned ourselves, and we find these kind of marriages work very well."

Dallas shook her head. "Jane doesn't know about his fiancée," she said quietly. "No matter what you may think, she really believes she loves Paris."

"She is bemused by his possessions," retorted Alexander Stavros, roughly. "Good God, I did not know there were such creatures left in the world today." He poured himself a strong whisky, and turned back to her. "You really are unique, Miss Collins, and I'll drink to that."

Dallas's cheeks burned. He was mocking her and she did not like it.

Apparently he had tired himself of baiting her, for he walked over to Myron Saravanos who was standing by the window, smoking quietly, and they had a short but animated conversation in Greek. Then Myron Saravanos left the room and Alexander Stavros lifted the telephone.

Dallas took little notice of what was going on around her. She thought that perhaps she ought to ring Charles, but he would not take kindly to being woken at seven a.m. on a Sunday morning, so she decided against it.

Time slipped by. She was aware that investigations were being carried out, trying to find the whereabouts of the missing couple, and Stephanos Karantinos appeared and spent some time talking to Stavros.

At ten-fifteen the telephone rang, and Alexander Stavros answered it himself. As he listened to what was being said his face darkened and he gnawed at his bottom lip for a moment before replying in the affirmative and replacing the receiver meticulously. Dallas could see his face was very pale beneath the tan, and Stephanos put a hand on his arm and spoke to him in his own language. Alexander Stavros answered him, and Stephanos gave a startled gasp and pressed his hands together violently, shaking his head. Dallas felt her nerves jumping. What now? She rose from her seat, and Stavros faced her wearily.

"They have been found," he said in an expressionless voice. "Paris is dead. Your sister is all right."

Dallas stared at him in bewilderment. "Paris is *dead*!" she echoed faintly. "But . . . I mean . . . how . . . ?"

Stavros shook his head. "As usual Paris was driving recklessly. He crashed into a lorry on the M1. Mercifully your sister was thrown clear. She is merely suffering from shock, and a few minor cuts and bruises." He lit a cheroot with hands that were not quite steady. "The police want me to go and identify the body of my son."

He turned away, clenching his fists, and Dallas looked from Myron Saravanos to Stephanos Karantinos awkwardly. She did not know what to do; what to say. Anything would sound inadequate. Stephanos took pity on her.

"Come, Miss Collins, I will take you home. Arrangements will be made to bring your sister back to you. I think you had better leave it all in our hands, yes?"

Dallas nodded, casting a compassionate glance at Alexander Stavros's back. What a terrible thing to have happened to him!

How desperately he must feel the pain.

She walked to the door, and then went out without speaking again. There was nothing she could say that would in any way assuage his grief. Besides, at times like these, it was his wife he needed most.

But when, in the car, she tentatively mentioned this to Stephanos Karantinos, he shook his head.

"Alex has no wife," he said softly. "She died almost ten years ago."

"Oh!" Dallas bent her head. "I'm sorry. I didn't know."

"How could you?" He shrugged. "Anna suffered from leukaemia. The last few months of her life she was in terrible pain. It was a blessed relief."

"Does . . . does Mr. Stavros have other children?"

"No. Paris was his only child."

"How terrible!" Dallas clasped her hands together in her lap. "So now he has no one."

"Not exactly," replied Stephanos, turning into the road where the girls' flat was situated. "He has a mother, and several brothers. He will not be completely alone."

He halted the sleek car, and Dallas slid out without waiting for his assistance.

"Well, thank you," she said. "Please let me know if there is anything I can do."

Stephanos nodded kindly, wished her good-bye, and drove away.

Dallas walked tiredly up the steps and into the flat. She felt shivery and shaky with the aftermath of the shock, and could hardly take it all in. It scarcely seemed possible that so much could have happened in such a short period. That Paris Stavros should be dead seemed incredible, and she wondered what the gossip-hungry press might make of it all.

She made herself some coffee, lit a cigarette, and sank down into a low armchair to await for Jane's return. Her thoughts were in a turmoil, and it was difficult to assimilate the events of the last few hours.

Charles would have to be told, of course, but she would leave that until later. Just now, she had no desire to be forced into revealing situations which were so painfully evident.

She needed time to gather herself together to speak to him, but for the moment she could only remember Alexander Stavros's face when he told her the news, all arrogance gone, leaving his face strangely vulnerable.

*   *   *

57

In the days immediately following the accident, Jane and Dallas acquired a closeness which they had not experienced since the first few months after their father's death. Jane seemed to have lost all her independence and clung to Dallas helplessly, looking to her for strength and guidance.

Alexander Stavros himself brought Jane home, carrying her up the stairs and into the flat as though she was a featherweight. His face had resumed its mask of indifference, although his eyes were strangely gentle as he looked at Jane.

Dallas indicated that he should leave her on her bed in the bedroom, and after he had done so and said goodbye to Jane, he came out, closing the door behind him to speak to Dallas alone.

His height and presence seemed to fill the small room, and Dallas, for all her five feet six inches, felt small and inadequate beside him.

"Are you all right?" he asked, looking down at her with his intensely dark eyes.

Dallas felt suddenly disturbed, and looked away from him.

"I . . . I . . . of course I am. Are . . . are you?"

He shrugged. "My feelings are not easy to describe," he replied, softly. "But yes, I suppose you could say I am all right."

"There's nothing I can say," began Dallas, twisting her hands together nervously.

"No, there is not." He took out his case and extracted a cheroot. "May I?" and at her swift nod, he lit it. "You will need to talk with your sister," he went on. "There is much to discuss."

Dallas didn't quite understand this remark, but she let it go. This was not the time for questions, and while she wished he would go with one half of her, the rest of her being experienced a desire for him to stay. He emanated a feeling of power and competence, and she thought he was the kind of man a woman would always feel protected with.

"So." He walked to the door slowly. "I will go. I have much to do . . . to arrange. We will of course see you later."

"Yes, Mr. Stavros," Dallas nodded hastily.

Brushing past him, she opened the door of the flat for him, but he stopped her, his eyes intent upon her.

"Dallas," he said, surprisingly, "I may call you that, may I not?"

Dallas nodded, too surprised to do anything else.

"Don't worry . . . about anything." He fastened the dark astrakhan coat closely about him, turning up the collar.

Dallas frowned. She didn't understand what he meant, unless he thought Jane was going to be very difficult to console.

"All right," she said, allowing him to open the door wide and step into the aperture. "Th . . . thank you, for bringing Jane home."

He nodded. "Oh, by the way, Dallas, don't be surprised if you find some newshounds on your doorstep later in the day. Unfortunately it will be impossible to keep something like this private. Do you understand? My life has been in the public eye for so long it is difficult for me to do anything without it being reported, and this is news!"

"Yes, Mr. Stavros, I understand." Dallas swallowed hard, and he half smiled, and then turning, walked swiftly away towards the stairs.

Dallas closed the door and leaned back against it momentarily. Then the sound of Jane's choked sobbing coming from the bedroom aroused her from her reverie, and with a stiffening of her shoulders she walked briskly through to the bedroom.

★　　★　　★

For several days the flat was besieged by newspaper men and women, all wanting to know how Jane was, and about her relationship with Paris Stavros. Dallas refused to answer any questions and Jane was too distraught to care one way or the other. So everything was left to Dallas, and she was forced to take a week off work so that she could stay with her sister.

Charles was unsympathetic. He couldn't understand Dallas's attitude, and said so.

"Really, Dallas," he complained, "you're treating the whole affair as though it was a grand tragedy. I thought you'd be glad that it was over once and for all."

Dallas stared at him, aghast at his unfeeling words. "I would never, *never* wish this on anybody," she denied hotly. "Charles, surely you can find it in your heart to feel compassion. Jane's going through a terrible experience, and she isn't going to be helped by that kind of statement. All right, I know it's over, but she needs love now, and gentleness, not chastising."

"Did you find out where they were going?" he asked bluntly.

Dallas shook her head. "We've never discussed it, why?"

"Well, I'd certainly be interested to know."

Dallas sighed. "I expect we will know everything in time, when Jane feels capable of telling us. Until then, we don't question her."

Charles snorted, and went away in a huff, but for once Dallas didn't particularly care what he thought.

She read from the newspapers that Alexander Stavros had flown his son's body back to Greece for burial there, and she wondered whether indeed she would ever see him again. It seemed unlikely. There was no reason why he should care about what happened to them now, and their paths were never likely to cross in the normal course of events.

Two weeks after the accident Dallas began to get really worried about Jane's depression. It did not seem to be lifting at all, and she refused to talk about anything remotely connected with the events of the last few weeks. She had not as yet returned to work, although naturally Dallas had had to return to her teaching job at the school. Jane spent her time either in bed, or moping about the flat, and refused to go and see a doctor, even though the doctors at the hospital where she had been taken after the accident had advised her to see her own doctor before resuming work. She averred that she was perfectly all right, and would get better in her own good time.

One evening, when Dallas was leaving the school gates at four o'clock, she was surprised to see a huge black Mercedes parked near by, and as she passed it on her way to the bus-stop the nearside door opened, and Alexander Stavros slid out and confronted her. It was a cold evening in early April, and Dallas was muffled up in a headscarf and her sheepskin jacket, and compared to the immaculate elegance of his clothes she felt terribly untidy. But he merely smiled, rather sardonically, she thought, and said:

"Hello, Dallas. Get in, please. I want to talk to you."

Dallas hesitated, only momentarily, and then slid into the passenger seat while he walked lazily round the bonnet and slid behind the driving wheel. He was driving himself today, so they were alone.

He did not start the engine, but instead offered her a cigarette which she gratefully accepted, while her body relaxed in the warm, luxury of the car. He lit himself a cheroot, and then looked sideways at her.

"Well?" he said. "I have been in England exactly three days, yet you have not made any attempt to get in touch with me."

Dallas stared at him in a bewildered fashion, her cheeks turning pink. "I . . . I don't understand," she said awkwardly.

"No? And yet I did send a message round to the flat advising you of my return."

"You did?" Dallas felt like an idiot. What on earth was all this about now?

"Of course. Your sister took the message herself."

"She did?" Dallas shook her head. "Well, I'm afraid she didn't tell me. Did . . . did you want to see me?"

"Did I want . . . ?" His eyes narrowed slightly. "I think perhaps we must be talking at cross-purposes. Naturally, *you* would want to see me."

"I would?" Dallas bit her lip, desperately

trying to understand him. At last she gave up. "I'm sorry, Mr. Stavros, but I don't know what you're talking about."

Now it was his turn to look surprised. He studied her intently for a moment, as though weighing up whether she was telling him the truth, and then he shrugged. "Perhaps you don't at that," he murmured. "I should have made certain before I left that you were informed. It seems apparent that your sister is afraid to tell you herself."

Dallas's fingers clenched convulsively on the strap of her handbag. "What is she afraid to tell me?" she asked breathlessly, her eyes wide and dismayed.

Alexander Stavros's mouth twisted. "It seems I must again be the bearer of unhappy tidings; your sister is pregnant."

Dallas felt her stomach turn over, and she suddenly felt very sick. It wasn't that it was such a great shock; she had known instinctively that all was not right with Jane for a long time, but now that it was put into words so blatantly, she felt suddenly lost and helpless, with no one to whom she could turn. Except Charles, her emotions argued, but what would Charles think?

Stavros stared out of the car window at the

passing traffic, giving her time to collect her scattered wits. He smoked his cheroot slowly, and Dallas, her eyes drawn to him, relaxed a little at his calm acceptance of the situation. When he thought she was recovering, he looked at her with his dark, inscrutable eyes.

"I'm sorry I had to break it to you so bluntly," he said. "But it was the only way. Your sister knows, of course, and I was told at the hospital when I went to bring her home. They thought I already knew, you see." He sighed. "I told Jane to tell you at once, but obviously she found herself incapable of doing so. I also outlined an idea to her which I wanted you to think about, too."

Dallas drew deeply on her cigarette. "She has said nothing at all about anything personal, but I suppose this explains the withdrawal symptoms she is suffering from."

"Yes," he nodded. "So now everything is known to you I will tell you my suggestions, yes?" As she inclined her head as though in assent, he went on: "This child, when it is born, will be my grandchild, do you understand? It matters little to me whether your sister was going to marry my son, or otherwise. The child is all that is important; I cannot have my grandchild ignored by his own family, so I have suggested to your sister that she comes with me to Lexandros until the child is born."

Dallas stared at him in astonishment. "Lexandros?" she echoed.

"Yes. Lexandros is an island, my island. My home is there; I was born there, and so was Paris. It is right that Paris's child should be born there also."

"Now wait a minute," began Dallas, as her brain began functioning again. "This child may be your grandchild, but it will be Jane's child first of all."

"I agree. But what does a child like Jane want with a baby? Can she keep it? Can she support it? I think not, and definitely not in the way I could support it."

Dallas felt anger rising inside her at this arrogance. "Mr. Stavros," she said, controlling her temper with difficulty, "it's not for you to decide, but Jane. Besides, I doubt whether Jane would want to leave England, and live among strangers, at such a time."

"Alone, I would agree," he said smoothly, "but I also suggested that you should accompany her. Naturally, I would not expect her to be separated from her own sister at a time like this!"

Dallas was astounded. "But I have a job!" she exclaimed, angrily now. "I couldn't just throw up my job and go to *Greece*. It's ludicrous. In any case, I'm getting married at the beginning of August."

"Indeed?" He looked thoughtful. "And is your sister's happiness at this time less important than your own?"

Dallas compressed her lips for a moment. "No, of course not. But that situation doesn't arise. Naturally I, and my fiancé, will take care of her, and the baby also when it comes."

"Your fiancé, what does he do?" queried Stavros coldly.

"He . . . he's an accountant," said Dallas shortly.

"And how will he react to this situation?" Stavros asked sardonically. "Is he the kind of man to be able to accept a young sister-in-law who is in quite a dilemma? Will he be prepared to support both you and Jane, and this baby when it arrives?"

Dallas stubbed out her cigarette in the ashtray. "That's our own affair," she prevaricated, unable to answer him truthfully, knowing Charles's attitude towards Jane, and of his mother's reactions when she heard the news.

"I think not," returned Stavros icily. "This is my affair, also. I, as Paris's father, have some rights."

Dallas's cheeks burned. "What do you mean?" she asked shakily. "Are you threatening us? Do I take it that you will use your money and influence to overrule any decisions we might care to make?"

Stavros's face was cold and hard as granite. "How dare you speak to me like that?" he exclaimed savagely, his accent more pronounced than she had ever heard it before, outlining to her more clearly than anything that he was not coolly English, but vibrantly Greek.

Dallas felt nervously aware of her own limitations, but she refused to be intimidated. "Well, isn't that what you meant?" she countered.

"No, damn you, it is not! Very well, *Miss Collins*, speak to your inestimable fiancé, and consider the ways and means, and I will contact you again after you have had time to come to your senses."

Dallas made to get out, but he put a staying hand on her arm. "I will drive you home," he said, in a low, controlled voice, but Dallas shook her head.

"That is not necessary," she said coldly.

"I think it is," he muttered, and drove away before she had a chance to get out of the car.

He halted at the flats, and Dallas slid out with alacrity, but he slid out too, and blocked her way for a moment.

"Remember," he said quietly, "that your sister is not wholly to blame. I blame myself and I blame Paris, although he cannot defend himself, and that is why I am prepared to take this child away before it has a chance to spoil your sister's life."

"Tell me," said Dallas suddenly, "what did Jane say when you told her?"

"I do not recall that she said anything," he replied. "She was too ill, too distraught to think seriously."

"I see." Dallas was allowed to proceed on her way, but she looked back at him. "Are you going back to Greece soon?"

"Not for three weeks," he replied quietly. "You will have plenty of time to change your mind."

"But . . ." Dallas began, then changed her mind, and with a nod she left him.

CHAPTER THREE

"BUT, Jane, honestly, why didn't you tell me?" Dallas walked slowly across the floor of the lounge, trying to compose to herself what she intended to tell Charles. "It isn't as though we haven't been close these last couple of weeks, is it? I mean, you've had plenty of time."

Jane lay on the couch, sipping a cup of coffee. She looked considerably more relaxed now than Dallas had seen her for weeks, and she felt a sense of contrition that Jane should have been unable to tell her own sister.

"I'm sorry, Dallas," she said, at last. "I wanted to tell you. That's why I've been so miserable, but I thought . . . well, after all, you were always warning me against Paris, weren't you, and this merely proved that you had been right all along."

"Oh, Jane, not necessarily." Dallas twisted her fingers together. "I mean, did you think I would say 'I told you so'?"

Jane half smiled. "Well, maybe. Although . . ." Her voice trailed away.

"There's so much more to it than this. Mr. Stavros only knows the bare facts. He doesn't know the full story." Her voice broke a little and she composed herself with difficulty.

Dallas frowned, and sank down on to the couch beside Jane. "What do you mean, Jane? What more is there to know?"

Jane turned away, burying her face in the soft cushions. Dallas laid a hand on her shoulder. "Jane, Jane! Surely now you can tell me. Nothing more momentous than knowing you're pregnant could possibly happen now."

"Couldn't it?" Jane lay back on the cushions, shading her eyes with her arm. "I really think our positions have reversed now, Dallas. I feel so much older than you, somehow."

Dallas felt disturbed. She had thought, before Alexander Stavros broke his shattering news to her, that things might conceivably return to normal eventually, but looking at Jane now she doubted the truth of this supposition. Even without the advent of the child, Jane had changed, in a strange, indefinable way.

Now she said: "Jane, please trust me. Tell me, whatever else should I know?"

Jane shook her head. "I didn't say you should know. I merely think you ought to, before you start trying to make me see anything good in having this baby."

Dallas shook her head now. "Jane, stop talking in riddles! Is this to do with Paris again?"

Jane nodded. "Well, go on," said Dallas impatiently. "I want to know, whatever it is."

Jane ran a tongue over her dry lips. "Did . . . did you think Paris and I ran away to get married?"

Dallas flushed. "Well, the thought crossed my mind."

"Did you tell Alexander Stavros?"

"Well . . . we discussed it."

"But surely he was less convinced than you," said Jane dryly.

Dallas remembered Alexander Stavros's words very clearly. Her expression revealed her thoughts very lucidly, and Jane nodded glumly.

"Of course, he would know. He knows Paris better . . . or rather . . ." her voice broke again, "he did know Paris better than anyone else." She sighed. "Oh, Dallas, you don't know how difficult this is for me!"

"I'm trying to, darling," murmured Dallas gently.

"Anyway, it wasn't *marriage* that Paris had in mind at all," Jane sniffed miserably. "He . . . well, when I told him about the baby, he said he didn't want *me*! Particularly not pregnant, anyway. He already had a fiancée . . . in Greece! I was terrified. I couldn't tell you, and have you tell Charles. All I could think of was the smug look he would wear when he knew!"

"Oh, Jane!"

"Dallas, if it hadn't been for Charles, I'd have told you. But you know what he's like!"

"Yes, I know," Dallas nodded, wondering what was going to happen now. What would Charles's reactions really be? "Tell me, Jane, do you remember what Mr. Stavros said to you about the baby?"

"Some of it," said Jane thoughtfully. "He . . . he suggested that he should take control of the affair."

"And what was your reaction to that?"

"At the time, I couldn't think straight. But now I don't know—why? Did he say more about it?"

"Oh yes. He seems to think he has every right to take the child and bring it up as his grandson, or granddaughter, as the case may be."

Jane nodded. "I know. I . . . I can see his point. After all, he has lost Paris, and he was his only offspring."

"Y . . . e . . . s," said Dallas, rather more thoughtfully. "But would you want to go to Greece to live, until after the baby is born?"

"To Greece?" echoed Jane. "No! What has Greece to do with it?"

"Well, that was Mr. Stavros's idea, wasn't it? He told me he wanted you to go and live on his island until afterwards. So that he can keep an eye on you, I suppose."

"Well, I don't remember that. In any case, I wouldn't go. To go and live among strangers, at a time like this. No, thanks!"

"But he said I should go, too," admitted Dallas reluctantly.

"I see," Jane grimaced. "Well, anyway, I don't think that's a good idea. He can have the baby, I suppose, but . . ."

"Jane, don't say things like that until you're sure that's what you want. This child is going to be yours as well. You might find you don't want to give it away."

"I couldn't afford to keep it, though, could I?" said Jane glumly. "Oh, what a mess!"

"Well, maybe you could keep it," murmured Dallas tentatively. "I mean, Charles and I are getting married soon. We could help you until afterwards, and then maybe support you until the child is old enough to go to a day nursery."

Jane stared at her. "Would you do that for me?"

"Of course. Oh, Jane, don't let's argue about this. It's over now, there's nothing we can do to stop it, so let's try and accept it."

"I think you're being overly optimistic, anyway," said Jane. "Charles won't agree to that in a million years."

"He might."

"Not a chance. Anyway, you know perfectly well that what Mrs. Jennings says goes. And she hates me!"

"She doesn't *hate* you," protested Dallas. "It's just that she is old, she's set in her ways. She doesn't understand young people. . . ."

"I know, I know. But what you can't seem to grasp is that Charles is like her. He's more like her contemporary than her son! Why, he even talks like she does. That's why you worry me sometimes, Dallas. You're only twenty-two. Can you afford to give up everything to live with

Charles? Your life will become complete domination."

"Oh, stop it!" Dallas got up and walked across the room biting the knuckles of one hand unsteadily. "We must work this out sanely and sensibly. There's no earthly reason why Charles can't help us, and I'm going to see him, and tell him everything."

Jane shrugged, pulled a face, and stretched out fully on the couch. "All right, Dallas, have it your way. It just may be that I am as adept at telling your fate as you were at telling mine."

★　　★　　★

The following Saturday evening, Charles called as usual to take Dallas down to Maidenhead. The weather was picking up now and Dallas wore a slim-fitting trouser suit belonging to Jane. It had been Jane's suggestion, a kind of veiled attempt to dare her into rebelling against Charles's influence on her clothes, and Dallas, wanting to appear confident, had agreed to wear the suit. It was royal blue corded velvet, with a flared line to the jacket, and suited her admirably. If anything she looked younger than her twenty-two years, despite the fact that her hair was in its usual french knot.

Charles did not say anything to her in the flat, but once in the comparative privacy of his Rover 2000 he gave vent to his feelings.

"Have you taken leave of your senses?" he queried coldly. "You know how I abhor women in trousers. Mother will have a fit when she sees you."

Dallas straightened her shoulders. "It's modern, Charles, and after all this is 1969, not the Victorian era!"

"You've never worn anything like that before. Have you bought it?"

"No. It's Jane's."

"Thank heaven for that!" Charles raised his eyes heavenward for a moment. "You're not the type for that kind of outfit."

"What am I the type for, Charles?"

Charles was taken aback. "Well, I don't know!" he blustered. "I mean you've always looked all right before."

Dallas stared out of the car window at the passing concrete slabs, inset with plate glass, which provided homes for thousands of people. This was hardly the way to get him into a good mood, she thought stupidly. Antagonising him from the beginning! She ought to have ignored Jane's tormenting tongue, and dressed to please him. As it was, Jane had provided the suit, so Jane would not be in Charles's good books. She sighed, and turned to look at him again. She might as well get it over with. It was no use waiting until they arrived when she would have to tell her story to his mother as well and suffer her critical remarks.

"Charles," she began quietly, "I . . . I have something to tell you. To . . . to ask you, too."

Charles negotiated a roundabout. "Oh yes?" he said coolly.

"Yes. It's about Jane."

Charles glanced at her. "Go on."

"She's pregnant."

A stony silence was maintained for several minutes while Dallas tried desperately to think of something to say. Anything to break down the barrier which Charles was erecting between them.

At last he said: "So she is, is she? Hard luck!"

"Is that all you have to say?"

Charles snorted, "What more is there?" He waved a car past them. "What's she going to do? Have the kid adopted?" He laughed.

"How ironic! Her passport into the millionaire class has been denied her!"

"That's a hateful thing to say!" exclaimed Dallas hotly.

"Well, what do you expect me to say? Poor old Jane! What a pity? No fear. She's mocked me long enough. Now it's my turn. And she won't get a dime out of it!"

This seemed to amuse him, and Dallas felt furiously angry.

"You couldn't be more wrong," she said coldly. "Alexander Stavros wants her to go to Greece and stay with them until the baby is born."

Charles stared at her, almost colliding with a stationary lorry.

"What!"

"Yes. That surprises you, doesn't it? However, Jane doesn't want to go, and leave everything that's known to her at a time like this. I've said we'll take care of her. After all, she is my sister——"

"That's out!" said Charles sharply. "I'm supporting no illegitimate kid of hers."

"I'm not suggesting you should," exclaimed Dallas angrily. "There's no reason why Jane shouldn't work as long as she can, and then there are grants, benefits, and afterwards, when the baby is old enough to go to a day nursery. . . ."

"Hold on, hold on!" Charles pulled off the motorway into a lay-by. "Where is she going to live all this time?"

"Well, primarily at the flat, and then when we get married, with us."

"Oh no, she's not." Charles shook his head. "That I will not have. I could put up with her maybe for a while in the ordinary way, but I'm having no unmarried mother living in my house. What would the neighbours think? And if the press get hold of this, as they're bound to sooner or later, it would be murder!"

Dallas stared at him as though she had never seen him before. She had known he was conservative, but she had never thought him to be so narrow-minded, or so petty.

"You can't be serious, Charles," she exclaimed, aghast.

"Oh, can't I?" Charles hunched his shoulders.

Dallas fumbled in her handbag for her cigarettes, and lit one with trembling fingers, careless of the fact that Charles disliked the car filled with smoke.

"Well," she began unsteadily, "if you're

serious, there's nothing more to be said, is there?"

Now it was Charles's turn to look uncomfortable.

"What do you mean?"

"Simply this. Where Jane goes, I go, or alternatively where she can't go, I can't go either."

"Now, stop talking nonsense," exclaimed Charles irritatedly. "What your sister does is her concern. Besides, you haven't given me a chance to say anything so far as Jane's welfare is concerned. I naturally don't expect you to abandon her."

"Thank you," said Dallas sarcastically. "That's good of you."

"Stop it, Dallas." Charles sniffed. "No, I think I have a plan. Jane can stay with you until our wedding, of course, but afterwards she can stay at one of these hostels until the baby is due. Then we can pay for her to go away to a nursing home and have the baby, and after it's adopted I shall have no objections to her coming to stay with us for a time."

"What if she doesn't want to have the baby adopted?"

"What do you mean? Of course she'll want

it adopted. No girl of seventeen wants to be saddled with a child and no husband."

"I agree to that, but most girls find it terribly difficult to part with their children. I thought we could help her there. . . ." .

Charles turned away, controlling his temper with difficulty. "I'm not going to have my life ruined by a slip of a girl," he said grimly. "And that's what will happen, make no mistake about it. Mother would never agree, anyway."

Dallas compressed her lips to stop them trembling. Like Jane she had been afraid of this, but even then she had repeatedly told herself that Charles was not as black as Jane painted him. Even now she was trying to find reasons for his attitude, but it was awfully difficult to feel anything but frustration in the face of his disregard for Jane's feelings.

"You're talking as though Jane were a stranger," she said, biting her lips. "She's my sister. I . . . I can't expect her to face this alone, without my support."

"Why not? She didn't much care what you thought when she was going out with him."

"I know she's been selfish and irresponsible, but Charles, she's my sister, and I love her."

"Well, I can't," said Charles flatly. "It's no good, Dallas. It would never work. We'd be at each other's throats in a month."

"So where does that leave me?"

"You must decide," replied Charles. "Me, or Jane."

Dallas stared at him. "That's a callous thing to say!"

"But true." It was obvious from his attitude that Charles thought she would give in, choose marriage with him above everything else. But Dallas couldn't do it, any more than he could love Jane. And some small voice, deep inside her, was saying: "Isn't it better to find out now than afterwards? When you're married to him? And can you honestly say you're heartbroken by the prospect?"

"Then I must choose Jane," said Dallas quietly.

Charles looked startled. "What!"

"You heard what I said perfectly well," replied Dallas. "It's no good for me either, Charles I could never live with you, not knowing where Jane was, or what she was doing."

"I never said that."

"No, but you said you wouldn't associate

with her while she was expecting this baby. I can see us having a terrible time if I want to see her and you don't. It's no good, Charles. I'm sorry, but there it is. I think you're the one who has made the decision, and you've chosen your mother."

Charles grunted angrily, "Dallas, you infuriate me! You're deliberately trying this on. I can't believe you could give up everything we've worked for these last few years at the drop of a hat, so to speak. That's simply not like you!"

"Have you ever wondered whether I am all you think I am?" asked Dallas, surprisingly. "I mean, you say that's not like me. Maybe it is. Maybe the person you know is not like me."

"You're talking rubbish, and I won't listen to any more of it." Charles started the car violently, and throwing it into the wrong gear stalled the engine at first attempt. Furious with himself, he started again, and Dallas wished she was in London, and able to get home alone. She looked round.

"Look, Charles," she said, "there's no point in my going to your mother's now. We have nothing more to say to each other."

"I disagree," muttered Charles, fumbling for his gears.

Dallas slid swiftly out of the car, looking about her thoughtfully. She might be lucky enough to catch a bus home. If not, she would rather walk than stay with Charles any longer just now.

Charles wound down the nearside window and glared out. "Dallas! Get back in the car this minute!"

Dallas turned away. "It's no good, Charles. I've told you!"

"Dallas!" Charles's tone turned to a plaintive one. "Dallas, please. Don't be so hasty. Let's talk some more about it."

"No. It's just no good Charles, and I can see no point in labouring on about it. Just let me go. I'll get the bus home."

Charles snorted furiously, "Very well, then, if you persist in being stupid about it. But I shall expect to hear from you. You know the number."

Dallas did not reply. There was nothing more to say.

★   ★   ★

Although Dallas told Jane what had happened between herself and Charles when she got back to the flat she did not invite con-

86

fidences, so Jane refrained from making any comment. But as the week progressed and Dallas became restless and moody, Jane had to have it out with her.

"Dallas, are you sure that's really what you want to do?" she asked sympathetically. "I mean, Charles was your choice, not mine, and it's no good breaking with him, whatever his views, if you love him."

Dallas ran a hand over her hair, shrugging her slim shoulders.

"That's just the trouble," she said, sighing. "Charles was my choice, and obviously a wrong one, because quite honestly I'm not brokenhearted about our separation. What's worrying me is what we're going to do now."

Jane traced a pattern on the arm of the chair she was sitting in.

"We . . . well, we could accept Alexander Stavros's offer," she murmured tentatively.

Dallas stared at her. "Are you serious?"

"Well, I only thought . . . I mean . . . he did say you could go, too, didn't he? And it would only be until the baby was born."

"No." Dallas shook her head. "That's the last thing we must do. If once he gets control of you, the child will never be yours again."

Jane frowned. "Why do you distrust him so? Surely, he seemed all right to me. I rather liked him."

Dallas lifted her shoulders. "It's just . . . his attitude! He's very arrogant."

"Well, of course he would be, wouldn't he?" exclaimed Jane. "A man in his position could hardly be anything else."

"Well, anyway, I'd rather we managed alone. Wouldn't you?" Dallas looked hopefully at her sister. "You know you can rely on me."

"I know." Jane smiled. "All right. I'm thinking of going back to work next week. No one need know. Nothing reveals my condition, and I'll leave before it's obvious."

Dallas nodded, but she wondered whether Jane really wanted to go back to work in those offices where they had all known about Paris, and would be avid for information.

Two days later she was summoned into the headmistress's office just before the lunch-break. Entering Miss Chater's office, Dallas wondered anxiously whether she was answering some sort of complaint against her. She hoped not at this time when she most particularly needed the security of her job.

But to her astonishment Miss Chater was not in the office when she arrived, and instead a tall dark man was awaiting her, rising from his seat at her entrance.

"You!" she exclaimed in astonishment, looking into Alexander Stavros's dark eyes.

"Good morning, Dallas," he said easily. "I'm sorry to intrude on your working hours, but I have an appointment this evening which I do not wish to break."

"Yes?" Dallas's voice was remarkably cool, considering she had burning cheeks, and a fluttering sensation in the region of her stomach.

Alexander Stavros walked towards her, thoughtfully, and then said: "I have been in contact with your . . . er . . . fiancé, or should I say ex-fiancé."

"You've what!" Dallas was astounded.

"Yes. I wished to make certain of his views on this rather delicate situation. I knew that you would be hardly likely to convey to me any worries you might have, and therefore I am afraid I intervened."

Dallas accepted a cigarette from him before speaking. "I don't see why you can't leave us alone," she said unsteadily. "I've told you, I'm quite capable of looking after Jane myself."

"Yes, I know. Unfortunately, I do not believe you. And nor do I believe that you are being wholly fair to your sister. I think you are allowing your antagonism towards me, and towards Paris, influence your decision. It is possible that Jane will fall in with your plans because she feels an acute sense of guilt about what she has done."

Dallas hunched her shoulders, unwillingly remembering Jane's suggestion that they should accept Alexander Stavros's offer, and her own outright rejection of any association with him.

Alexander Stavros looked down at her enigmatically. "What is wrong? Do you really feel I might be right? Be honest with yourself. Admit you may be wrong!"

Dallas looked up at him. "I . . . I think it's possible that Jane would go to your island, but what of me? I couldn't possibly go, and I doubt very much whether she would go without me."

"I doubt this also. So far as your job is concerned there is no earthly reason why you cannot leave it."

"We shall need money," exclaimed Dallas, half angrily. "You seem to be forgetting that."

"On the contrary, I never forget money," he replied suavely. "However, I do not believe money enters into this at all. You cannot imagine that I would expect you to live on Lexandros penniless!"

"We don't want your money!" exclaimed Dallas scornfully. "I wouldn't take a penny of it."

"Oh, grow up, *Miss Collins!*" he snapped violently. "How old are you? Twenty, twenty-two, perhaps? I don't know. You are behaving like a foolish schoolgirl. Jane is entitled to support from the father of her child, and I am perfectly prepared to admit that Paris was that man. This being so, I as his father am entitled to financially take his place. Jane must recognise this if you do not. Stop behaving so childishly. If you cannot come to Lexandros in any other capacity then I will *invent* a job for you, for which I can pay you a salary."

"That's ridiculous!" Dallas turned away.

She felt his hands grip her arms, swinging her back round to face him. "No one turns their back on me!" he muttered savagely. "Least of all a woman!"

Dallas shivered, and he let her go. "So!" he said icily. "That is my decision."

Dallas shook her head. "It's not yours to make."

"Oh, but it is, Miss Collins. Just watch me!" He swore in his own language. "For God's sake, be reasonable. I can help you. No one is more willing to do so. At least give Jane the chance to decide for herself!"

"Then let Jane go, if that's what she wants," said Dallas shortly.

"No. You know she will refuse to go alone. Either you agree to go also, or Jane will give all this up, all we can do for her, because of you!"

It was an impossible situation. Dallas was beaten before she started. Hadn't she already got proof that Jane was willing to go if she was?

"You're making it impossible for me to refuse," she said, biting her lips. "I think you're despicable!"

"And you are naïve and immature," he replied unkindly. "And so far as your feelings towards me are concerned I can safely say that they will not matter much, one way or the other."

Dallas sank down on to Miss Chater's chair. "All right, Mr. Stavros, you win. I'll see what Jane has to say. But there's still my work to be considered. . . ."

92

"You are free in ten days," he remarked coolly, lighting a cheroot, which seemed to be all he ever smoked.

Dallas's eyes widened. "I'm what?"

"I took the liberty of discussing this matter with Miss Chater, before you arrived," he replied suavely. "Naturally, she had to be told the facts, or some of them, at least—in confidence, of course."

"You were so sure we would go!" exclaimed Dallas, feeling hot and frustrated.

"Reasonably. As you said, I did not leave you much choice. However, I hope you will find that the situation is not as black as you seem to think it. Lexandros is quite an enchanting island, and you will find plenty to do to fill your days. The swimming is very good, and of course, there are sports of all kinds."

Dallas fingered the pleat in her skirt. "I would prefer to think there was something I could do; I'm not by nature a sybarite!"

"And you think I am?"

"Well, aren't you?" she countered, not looking at him.

"No, Miss Collins, I am not. However, as you seem determined to cause difficulties, I will endeavour to find you some kind of occupation."

93

Dallas inclined her head, and then stood up. "Is that all?"

"For the moment." He looked angry momentarily at her deliberately off-hand manner, and then he smiled, revealing even white teeth, the smile transforming his face from sombre saturninity to mockingly amused satisfaction. He placed the cheroot between his teeth, fastening his overcoat, and speaking as he did so: "You will find, Miss Collins, that circumstances can change identities. We are on your ground at the moment, and you feel capable of crossing swords with me without fear of counter-attack. Maybe when you reach Lexandros you will find the situation somewhat different. Do you feel you will be able to meet this challenge?"

Dallas pressed a hand to her stomach nervously. "I don't know what you mean," she said, trying to sound nonchalant and not quite succeeding.

"Don't you? I think you do. I have known many women, Miss Collins, and I feel that has given me a little knowledge on the subject."

"Your personal life doesn't interest me," said Dallas rudely. "May I go now?"

His eyes narrowed, but she was no longer annoying him, and she could only assume that now he had got his own way on the matter of them going to Greece he could afford to be expansive. She didn't actually know why she was behaving like this; she had never thought of herself as being small-minded or petty, and yet she was allowing this arrogant Greek to get under her skin and he knew it.

"Yes, you can go," he said lazily, walking to the door and opening it for her. "My secretary will be in touch with you to make all the necessary arrangements."

"Which one?" asked Dallas childishly.

"Well, as I have about half a dozen, I am sure I can spare someone," he replied sardonically. "Thank you, and goodbye, Miss Collins."

Dallas walked out feeling quite idiotic. Why had she had to make that final stupid remark? He would think her quite ridiculous. And so she was, behaving like this, but his overbearing manner infuriated her, and knowing he was making them do what he wanted was humiliating when for the past three years she had made all the decisions.

She went back to her class feeling disturbed, and quite incapable of teaching them anything.

CHAPTER FOUR

ONCE Jane knew that it was settled, and that they were going to Lexandros, she brightened up considerably, and Dallas had to assume that Alexander Stavros had been right; Jane had felt distressed and guilty about the whole affair.

As for Dallas, she had to accept defeat gracefully, although the prospect of the next few months among strangers filled her with dismay. Although she worked with children, she was still rather shy, and she wondered however she was going to adapt herself to meeting the Stavros family.

The next couple of weeks were filled with shopping, arranging about letting the flat in their absence, and getting all the necessary forms to take them to Lexandros. Stephanos Karantinos was continually in touch with them, and he arranged all travelling details. Alexander Stavros had returned to Greece, and Dallas was relieved. At least it seemed they were not going to have to travel with him.

Two days before they were due to leave, Charles telephoned Dallas at work. This was an unheard-of procedure for him, he would never ring her during working hours normally, but this was different, he said.

"You can't be seriously leaving without seeing me again," he exclaimed peevishly.

"So you know we're leaving?" replied Dallas coolly.

"Of course. That . . . that Alexander Stavros made it pretty clear that there would be no question of you doing otherwise."

"What!"

"Yes. He said that it didn't matter whether I could support you both or not, your place was with him as it's his grandchild."

Dallas gripped the phone tightly. "He said that!"

"Yes. I . . . I wanted to ring you before, but as he had advised me to leave it all to him . . ." He halted. "You do want to go, don't you, Dallas?" His tone was plaintive, deliberately, but Dallas was too angry to wonder at Charles's change of attitude.

"I'll ring you later," she said, putting down the telephone receiver with suppressed violence. She felt furiously angry, and for the moment her emotions ruled her head.

She reported to Miss Chater that she had something to do, and uncaring of Miss Chater's annoyance she collected her coat and left the school. She took a taxi to the Dorchester Hotel where Stephanos Karantinos was still staying and after the usual preliminaries she was admitted to the suite. Stephanos came through from the bedroom, fastening the buttons of his shirt as though he had just got up. As it was already ten-thirty in the morning, Dallas felt an unreasonable anger at the sight of him.

His grey eyes appraised her lazily, and then he said: "All right, Dallas, what's wrong?"

Dallas's eyes were flashing. "You can tell your *so-powerful* boss that we are not going to Lexandros after all!"

Stephanos stared at her, and then lifting a tie from the back of a chair, he slid it round his neck.

"Why?" he asked, not creating any of the scenes Dallas had envisaged.

Dallas was momentarily taken aback. "It's . . . it's a personal matter, between Alexander Stavros and me."

"Is it?" Stephanos's eyes were openly amused now.

Dallas flushed. "Yes! Oh, what's the use? Anyway, give him the message."

"You can give it to me, instead!"

Dallas almost jumped out of her skin. She had thought they were alone, but another man came walking into the room, tall and slim and dark, and younger than Alexander Stavros. His hair was tightly curled about his well-shaped head, and his eyes were laughing.

"Allow me to introduce myself," he went on. "My name is Nikos Stavros. I am Alex's brother."

Dallas had known that Alexander Stavros had brothers and sisters, but she had not thought of them as real people, whereas Nikos Stavros was very real and very attractive.

"This is Dallas Collins," said Stephanos, pulling on his jacket, "Jane's sister. Dallas, Nikos is here to escort you and Jane back to Lexandros."

Dallas ran a restless hand over her hair, and then stiffened her shoulders. "Well . . . well, that won't be necessary now, will it?"

"On the contrary," Nikos spoke. "Of course you are coming to Lexandros. Alexander will . . . how do you say it? . . . murder me, if I go back without you." He grinned. "Now you couldn't allow that to happen, could you, Dallas?"

Dallas turned away. It was obvious that they simply were not going to take her seriously. "There's nothing more to be said," she replied coldly, despite the appeal in Nikos's eyes. "I meant what I said. I won't have your brother treating me like an imbecile."

"How has he done that?" asked Stephanos, walking across to her.

"I . . . I can't tell you."

"Yes, you can." Stephanos was serious now. "Come on, tell me."

Dallas hesitated. "Let me guess," said Stephanos quietly. "It has to do with Charles Jennings, has it not?"

Dallas was astounded. "How do you know that?"

Stephanos shrugged. "It is not difficult. Alex is a pretty shrewd judge of character. He has to be. He was afraid that this man might try to deter you."

"Charles merely told me that Mr. Stavros told him that we were going to Lexandros long before he had even consulted *me*!"

Stephanos shrugged. "I told you, Alex is a very good judge of character."

100

"And what about his own?" exclaimed Dallas angrily. "He's practically *blackmailed* us into going!"

Nikos intervened. "I will vouch for my brother's character any time you say," he said coolly. "I would not be willing to make this remark for anyone else, but Alex, yes." He smiled. "Come now, Dallas, do not be like this. Let us be friends. What has Alex done that is so terrible? I know that most girls in your position would be blessing their good fortune, not throwing tantrums because he has been a little . . . shall we say . . . pretentious?"

Dallas shrugged her shoulders, feeling suddenly dejected. As her anger subsided her common sense asserted itself and she knew that it didn't particularly matter now what Alexander Stavros had done; for Jane's sake she had to go.

"I'm not throwing tantrums," she said wearily.

Nikos glanced meaningly at Stephanos, and he quietly withdrew, leaving them alone. "Now," said Nikos, looking down at her, "surely the prospect is not such a bleak one. I mean, Lexandros is a marvellous place; and although I've been all over the

101

world, there's nowhere else I would rather call home."

Dallas looked at him through the thick veil of her lashes, and felt the colour burning in her cheeks at the look in his eyes. Nikos seemed disturbed by her nearness, and he murmured:

"You may find you actually enjoy it. It will be difficult not to do so when the men of Lexandros will all be charmed by your arrival." He smiled. "If your sister is like you your presence will certainly enliven our island."

Dallas turned determinedly away. "I must go."

"All right," Nikos nodded, and moved ahead of her to the door to open it for her. "And I do not have to telephone my brother that the matter requires his attention?"

"No." Dallas compressed her lips.

"Good. *Adio*, until Sunday."

★   ★   ★

The flight out to Lexandros was a memorable one for the two girls who had never flown by jet before. Even Dallas found it difficult to maintain her detachment when there was so much around her to intrigue and delight her. There were four of them on this flight; Stephanos and Jane, Nikos and herself. She was not aware who separated them into two pairs, but she found herself with Nikos at her side, and as he was an amusing companion she began to enjoy the trip enormously.

They landed at lunchtime in Athens, and ate a delicious meal in the airport restaurant before driving out to a smaller aerodrome where the Beagle belonging to the Stavros Shipping Line awaited them, to take them on the last leg of their journey to the island. "Lexandros does not have an airstrip long enough to take a jet," remarked Nikos casually, "or Alex would most certainly have had one by now. My brother does not believe in wasting time."

"That I can believe," replied Dallas dryly, looking back regretfully at the soaring white mass of the Acropolis standing on its mound above the historic city, just waiting to be explored.

Nikos grinned. "I see. You would have liked to see more of Athens." He glanced at Stephanos. "Would you like to take Jane ahead to the island, and Dallas and I will spend a couple of days at the Hilton, and take in some of the tourist spots.''

"Oh no!" Dallas was horrified. "I mean, Jane wouldn't want to go on alone, would you?" She looked at Jane appealingly.

Jane smiled. "Quite honestly I'm a mass of nerves. I couldn't go on alone, but contrarily, I don't think I could cope with much sightseeing."

Nikos nodded, and his smile was amused yet sardonic. "All right, we'll play it cool. I forget you are not an impulsive race as we are."

Dallas breathed a sigh of relief. Much as she would have liked to spend several days in Athens, she felt sure Alexander Stavros would not approve of too close a friendship with his brother, and besides, Nikos was too aware of his attraction and she felt strangely vulnerable now that she was free from Charles. The casual mention of the Athens Hilton brought home to her powerfully the immense difference in their backgrounds, as well. Even in the days when their father was alive they had stayed at small *pensions* on the few occasions when they were abroad.

The trip over the blue waters of the Aegean drove all other thoughts from the girls' minds. Looking down, they could see dozens of tiny islands interspersed among the larger ones, looking like jewels in sapphire satin. The occasional white sails of sloops or schooners added their own splash of brilliance, and it was with regret that Dallas realised they were banking slightly, ready to land on the island below them.

Jane pressed a hand to her stomach, and Dallas looked swiftly at her. "Are you all right?" she asked, at once.

Jane shook her head. "I just feel a bit sick," she admitted, looking a little pale. "Nerves, I suppose."

Nikos was looking thoughtful. "Please," he said, "do not be afraid. There is nothing to be afraid of." He shrugged. "You may find my mother a little intimidating at first, but soon you will come to love and admire her."

Dallas felt apprehensive. She hoped Mrs. Stavros would not turn out to be another Mrs. Jennings.

"How . . . how many brothers do you have?" she asked, looking down as they dropped lower towards the island.

Nikos seemed to be studying this question and Stephanos answered for him. "He is teasing you, pretending he does not know," he replied. "There are three more sons, beside Alex and Nikos, and four daughters. Two of Nikos's sisters are married, and also two of his brothers, this is in addition to Alex himself, who is of course a widower."

"So there are nine of you," exclaimed Jane, aghast. "What a large family!"

Nikos smiled mockingly. "We like large families, madonna."

Jane's face suffused with colour, and Dallas felt sorry for her, and yet perhaps it would do her good to speak about her baby more naturally.

The island seemed to be rushing up to meet them now and Dallas stared in wonder at the long stretches of sandy beach set in coves with curving headlands. It was outstandingly beautiful and she felt a strange ache in her throat. It was unspoilt, uncommercialised, and there seemed an abundance of greenery, thick foliage bounding down to the shoreline in places.

Inland a mountainous range seemed covered with trees of all kinds, and among the trees she glimpsed the sparkling whitewashed houses where many of the population lived. The airstrip was on the coast, near to a cluster of dwellings and a small harbour which was obviously the main point of the island.

"The fishing village of Lexa," murmured Nikos, in her ear, leaning across and following the line of her eyes.

Dallas glanced round at him, and for a moment their faces almost touched, and then she looked away again. Nikos blew softly on her ear, revealed by the upswept style of her hair which she had not changed despite Jane's pleas.

"I think I am going to enjoy this summer," he murmured softly, so that only she could hear, and Dallas moved as far across her seat as she could, conscious that Jane was watching them speculatively, a faint frown on her face.

"Don't you work?" Dallas asked, a little breathlessly.

"Sometimes," he said lazily, lying back in his seat, as though pleased with life at the moment.

The landing strip at Lexandros was surprisingly modern and well laid out, and Dallas could only assume that this was on account of its connection with the Stavros company. The plane taxied to a halt near the airport buildings, and the two girls allowed Nikos to precede them down the flight of steps to the runway below.

Jane took Dallas's arm tightly, and said: "Don't leave me with Stephanos again, Dallas. Stay with me. I know Nikos seems to have gone overboard for you, but that's not why we're here, is it?" Her tone was slightly peevish, and Dallas could only assume that the trip had been too much for her.

"I know why we're here," she said flatly, ignoring the hand that Nikos held out to help her down the last few steps, and turning instead helped Jane on to the ground.

There were plenty of lookers-on to their arrival. Children dressed in vividly coloured shorts and shirts were gathered in groups at the edge of the strip, giggling and laughing and pointing at the new arrivals. Several old men were seated outside the airport buildings, smoking and drinking the ubiquitous *ouzo* which seemed to be the most popular aperitif.

To the left of the strip, the ground sloped away towards a sandy shoreline, laced with palms, and beyond, the sparkling waters of the Aegean beckoned invitingly. The air was incredibly clear. Dallas had heard that this was so, but even she was not prepared for the clarity of the vista stretched like a backcloth before her fascinated eyes.

The cases were unloaded from the aircraft by two porters, and carried across the tarmac to a low-slung convertible, glistening in blue and chrome, which was parked by the gate. A slim young girl who was seated behind the wheel eyed them almost insolently as Nikos led them across, and then slid out indifferently to be introduced.

"This is my sister Natalia," murmured Nikos, giving Natalia a reproving glance. "Natalia, meet Dallas and Jane Collins."

Natalia nodded her head languidly, her heavy mane of black hair falling in curling ringlets around her slim shoulders. She looked about sixteen, but was obviously older to be driving. She was dressed in a very short pink skirt and a sun-top which left several inches of her midriff bare, and looked cool and assured.

"Hello, Natalia," said Dallas politely, refusing to be deterred by the other girl's unfriendly manner, while Jane merely acknowledged Natalia in much the same way as the Greek girl had acted.

Dallas hoped there was not going to be unconcealed antagonism from the rest of the

Stavros family, most particularly Madame Stavros, or their time on the island was not going to be very pleasant. Nikos had said they might find his mother intimidating earlier on, and Dallas felt her stomach muscles tense with nervousness. It was such an unreal situation, and one which she wished she had not got to experience.

Stephanos took over driving the car on the journey to the Stavros home. Natalia bestowed on him a most charming smile and Dallas thought that it was only themselves, she and Jane, with whom Natalia had any antagonism. Nikos seemed to notice nothing amiss, and smiling cheerfully assisted Jane and Dallas into the back of the open car, and then climbed in beside them. Natalia seated herself beside Stephanos, and with the cases safely stowed in the trunk they were off.

The road wound round the shoreline of the island, giving the girls ample opportunity to take in and admire the magnificent scenery. There were numerous small coves and inlets; some rocky promontories, and others soft and silkily sanded, caressed by the creaming surf. The profusion of greenery they had seen from the aircraft distinguished itself as groves of palms, clusters of fruit trees that Dallas recognised as orange and lemon, while the whole was embellished by the exuberant growth of every kind of flower imaginable from oleanders and jasmine to hibiscus and bougainvillea. The colours were startling, vivid reds and blues, yellows and pastel shades of every colour. Nikos identified the flowers for her, pointing out the beauty spots they passed, some overhung with blossoms, ruined temples looking like fairy-tale arbours, while the scents of the island surrounded them.

Nikos leaned forward, smiling at them. "It is as I said, is it not?"

Jane looked bemused. "I've never seen such a beautiful place," she admitted enthusiastically. "Does this all belong to your brother?"

Natalia glanced round, her eyes scornful suddenly. "Yes, it is all Alex's now. When our father died it passed to the eldest son, but it is the home of the Stavros family, which is more to the point." Her words were scathing, and Jane's cheeks turned bright red.

Nikos intervened before Jane could reply. "What Natalia is trying to say is that although the island is Alex's property, provision is always made for those members of our family who continue to live here."

"I think I know what Natalia meant," retorted Jane hotly. "She was implying that we have no right to be here."

"Not at all," exclaimed Nikos, before Natalia made another angry response. "Look, let's stop this, shall we? Alex is the boss and he invited you, and I for one am glad. Let's leave it at that!"

"Maria is my greatest friend!" stormed Natalia, not abashed by her brother's remarks.

"Who is Maria?" asked Dallas quietly, her stomach churning with the effort to keep calm.

"Maria was Paris's betrothed," said Natalia coldly. "How do you think she feels to have your sister coming here, expecting Paris's child, when she . . . when she . . ." Her voice broke, and she swung round in her seat so that they could not see her face.

Jane's cheeks were pale now. "I'm sorry," she said, clenching her hands together tightly in her lap.

Dallas felt terrible, and again she wished they had not come. This was going to be *awful*; this continual resentment and antagonism. If it persisted no matter what Alexander Stavros said, they would leave. She could see that Jane was on the verge of tears herself and she looked at Nikos, biting hard at her lips.

Nikos shrugged his shoulders eloquently, and then half smiled.

"Relax," he murmured softly, close to Dallas's ear so that only she could hear. "Brother Alex will soon deal with Natalia."

Dallas looked at him squarely. "Do you think we want to be here on those terms?"

"No. And you won't be. As I said, relax, honey."

Dallas wished it was that easy. But she couldn't rid herself of the fear that Alexander Stavros himself might have changed once away from the confines of England and back in his own country. Had she not already had proof that he could be cruel and unyielding, arrogant when his own wishes were tampered with? She really knew nothing about him, he was unpredictable.

They reached the far side of the island quite quickly, and down an incline, nestling among a grove of trees, its grounds reaching down to the edge of cliffs which protected a silvery-sanded cove, was the Stavros villa. Slightly above it like this they could see the well-laid-out grounds with a swimming pool glinting in the sunlight in the forecourt. It seemed an enormous place even from this distance, and although it was modern in conception its design of Grecian pillars and courtyards inset with tinkling fountains, melted unobtrusively into its surroundings.

Nikos smiled as he saw Jane's eyes widen as they turned between stone pillars and approached the house up a sweeping drive. Now the swimming pool was nearer they could see the mosaic-tiled surround, set about with airbeds and loungers, striped umbrellas protecting small tables from the heat of that already powerful sun. It was so much like a scene out of a Technicolor advertisement that even Dallas allowed herself a small gasp of pure enjoyment.

To the right of the house, a veritable forest of trees converged almost to the doorstep, while among the trees were small chalet-type dwellings which Nikos explained were used when they had several house-guests.

"At the moment there is only Maria Pengouste, and the Sharef family, but sometimes we have as many as twenty or thirty people staying here."

Dallas's heart sank as Nikos mentioned Maria Pengouste. She must be the girl

Natalia had spoken about. This was not going to be an easy sojourn.

The car halted at the side of the house and Nikos helped Dallas out while Stephanos again took charge of Jane. The cases were left for someone else to collect, and they entered the house through french doors into a low light lounge which ran from one side of the building to the other. It was deserted, but Nikos and Natalia both walked out through an arched doorway into what appeared to be the hall of the house.

Stephanos glanced at the girls thoughtfully. "Do not concern yourself with Natalia's remarks," he said softly. "She is young and hot-blooded, and intensely loyal to Maria. Unfortunately, she was unaware of Paris's penchant for the opposite sex. At home he acted impeccably. Only Alex knew the real Paris. You will need to exercise your own personalities here. That is the criterion by which you will be judged." He shrugged. "Maybe 'judged' is too strong a word. Do not be alarmed. In no time at all you will be accepted, believe me. Madame Stavros is the most charming of women. She will not allow guests in her house to be treated less than politely."

"Thank you." Dallas made an attempt at a smile. "It's all so strange. So opulent, so *rich*. However will we adapt?"

Stephanos grinned. "I was born in the back streets of Athens. I have achieved complete naturalisation. So will you. It takes time, that is all."

"Is . . . is Mr. Stavros here at the moment?" asked Dallas tentatively.

Stephanos shrugged. "I doubt whether he is actually in the house, but yes, he is on the island. Why?"

Dallas shook her head, and Jane glanced at her strangely.

Stephanos's eyes were shrewd. "Dahlia Sharef will be with him, wherever he is. You will meet them all at dinner this evening."

"Who is Dahlia Sharef?" It was Jane who spoke.

"She is the daughter of one of his business associates. Her mother and father are staying here at the moment, as Nikos said."

Dallas wondered why Stephanos had told her that. After all, what Alexander Stavros did was his own affair and no one else's. It seemed strange that Stephanos should think she might be interested, unless, and her heart skipped a beat, unless Stephanos was trying to tell her something. To warn her.

Her cheeks turned pink and she quickly moved so that Jane could not see her face. Did Stephanos imagine she was becoming interested in Alexander Stavros rather more than was necessary? And was he trying to tell her that he was not a man to take seriously? It seemed ridiculous, and yet Stephanos had not mentioned Dahlia Sharef for nothing. As if *she* would be interested in Alexander Stavros! It was ludicrous. Apart from anything else, she did not have ideas like that. He was far above her head, and after all, Jane was a prime example of what could happen if one attempted to play games with tigers.

Her thoughts were thankfully interrupted as Nikos returned to the room together with an elderly woman whom Dallas judged to be in her early sixties. She was tall and stately, dressed in a Crimplene suit of violet, a triple string of pearls, which Dallas supposed were real, about her throat. Her hair was wound on top of her head in a coronet of plaits and she had very piercing grey eyes. They were not so dark as her son's and in their depths Dallas could read no animosity. She breathed a little more easily while Nikos performed the introductions.

"Nikos tells me you have been travelling since early this morning," she said in faultless English, after Nikos had finished his introductions. "No doubt you are hot and tired. I will have you shown straight to your rooms, and we will serve you with a little English tea so that you may rest until dinner time."

"Thank you." Dallas managed a smile.

"The circumstances of your visit with us may be unconventional," Madame Stavros continued, "but you must make yourselves at home here, and try to enjoy your stay. The weather as you can see is perfect, and there is no reason why you should not treat this in the nature of a holiday. I have allotted you your own villa, in the grounds, and as they are self-contained it will not be necessary for you to come to the house for anything should you not desire to do so."

Dallas felt that this was a little more what she had expected. The iron hand in the velvet glove. They were being politely manoeuvred into a villa in the grounds; a compact self-sufficient building, from which they would not be encouraged to stray. She glanced at Jane, but Jane was merely beginning to feel the strain of the introductions, and felt she would be glad of a chance to lie down and relax, alone with Dallas.

"The girls are expected to eat with us, Mama," remarked Nikos quietly in his mother's ear. "Alex's instructions, yes?"

His mother compressed her lips momentarily. "Of course," she said, a little stiffly. "There is no reason why they should not do so. I merely thought I should explain that should they desire to remain in their own accommodation, arrangements can be made. . . ."

"I think we understand you, Madame," said Dallas abruptly. "Don't imagine we have any desire to intrude upon your lives here. We would much rather have stayed in England. Unfortunately, your son made that almost impossible. . . ."

"Yes, so I did," remarked a coolly amused voice.

Dallas swung round sharply to find Alexander Stavros leaning lazily against the arched doorway which led into the hall. He was dressed in close-fitting cream pants, and a navy blue knitted nylon sweater, unbuttoned at the neck so that the beginnings of the dark mat of hairs on his chest could be seen. With his dark hair slightly damp and tousled

119

as though he had been swimming, and the dark growth of a beard along his jawline, he looked considerably different from the immaculately dressed businessman that Dallas remembered seeing in London. He was infinitely more attractive this way; more approachable and consequently much more dangerous.

"Alex!" His mother swung round too. "I didn't know you were back."

"Obviously not," he remarked, straightening, and walking slowly towards them. "I thought I made my instructions perfectly clear. You may have your way, and accommodate the girls in a villa in the grounds as I feel that this is what they themselves would want, but, Mama, you will not try to shelve the responsibility for them as though they were not here. Do I make myself understood?"

His indolent manner did not in any way lessen the effect of his words and Madame Stavros looked slightly disturbed. "You know as well as I do, Alex——" she began, only to be silenced by the expression he wore. Then she lapsed into Greek, completely excluding Dallas and Jane from comprehension of what was transpiring.

Alexander Stavros listened to her thoughtfully for a moment, lighting a cheroot from a gold case which he had withdrawn from the pocket of his trousers. Then he shrugged, and smiled rather sardonically, and turning to Dallas said:

"You had a good journey? My brother looked after you?" His eyes turned to Jane as Dallas politely affirmed, and he enquired after her health, his dark eyes straying momentarily over the slender width of her young body. Then he looked at Dallas again, and there was challenge in his eyes as he said: "You will both come for dinner at nine o'clock. The servants will be on hand to give you any information you require. But now it is growing late and you must both wish to rest after your journey. Yanni!"

The peremptory tone of his voice brought a young man in white uniform to his side, and he issued instructions in Greek at which the young man nodded, and affirmed that he would carry out.

The girls wished their hostess *au revoir*, and accompanied Yanni outside again and across the width of luscious green turf to one of the whitewashed chalets among the trees some distance from the house. Dallas was too engrossed with her own thoughts to pay much attention to her surroundings, and the undercurrents of emotion at the house had disturbed her not a little. But once there she recovered and took delight in exploring the small dwelling which was to be their home for the next few months.

Yanni showed them around. There was a small lounge which could also be used as a dining-room, two bedrooms, each luxuriously furnished with double beds, and a bathroom with a step-in bath and shower, done out in the palest of pastel greens. It really was a miniature house, and Jane was enchanted and forgot for a moment the animosity they had experienced.

"It's marvellous!" she exclaimed. "Tell me, Yanni, do you speak English?"

Yanni smiled, his dark-skinned face beaming. "A little," he said. "If you speak slow, yes?"

Jane smiled also. "Then tell us about arrangements here. Dinner is at nine, so Mr. Stavros said. What time is breakfast?"

"Any time you like," said Yanni carefully. "There is no time set, you understand. Lunch is at two."

Dallas removed the jacket of her suit. She

was feeling uncomfortably warm and was looking forward to a cooling shower in that delightful bathroom.

"Perhaps Mr. Stavros will give us more details tonight," she said, trying not to sound concerned when she said Alexander Stavros's name.

Jane looked at her. "He looked different," she said thoughtfully. Then she remembered Yanni. "All right, Yanni, you can go. What do we do to get in touch with you again?"

"The bell," murmured Yanni politely, indicating a button on the wall beside the french windows. "*Adio*, Miss Collins, Miss Jane."

He withdrew, and Jane walked through to one of the bedrooms and flung herself lazily on the bed. Dallas followed her rather more slowly. Jane looked up as she entered.

"What do you think?" she asked bluntly.

Dallas shrugged. "It's like I expected. They don't really want us here. And why should they?"

"I do happen to be having Paris's baby," said Jane resentfully. "I'm sorry, but he was as much to blame as anyone."

"I know, darling." Dallas lifted her shoulders in a helpless movement. "But we can't expect them to fall over themselves to look after us. I half wish Mr. Stavros hadn't come in like that. I had no desire to eat in company with the rest of the family and their guests. Heavens, I'd rather they forgot we were here."

Jane made a moue. "Well, I don't," she said swiftly. "After all, we'll never have a chance like this to see how the other half lives ever again, will we?"

Dallas unfastened her hair from the french pleat and ran her fingers through its thick silkiness. "Well, anyway, we're not going to have a choice. I just wish I knew what I was going to wear."

"Why? You brought several suitable dresses," exclaimed Jane. "After all, we can't be expected to look like they do. We're only the poor semi-relations."

Dallas smiled. "All right. But now I'm going to have a shower. I feel absolutely sticky."

Jane nodded. "I'll have a rest, then. It's early yet. I'm quite looking forward to this evening, though. And to return to my point, didn't you think Alexander Stavros looked different?"

Dallas walked to the door, ignoring the way the blood pounded through her veins at the mention of his name. "He . . . well, he's grown a beard," she said lightly.

"Not only that. He seemed much younger, somehow. Gosh, he must be as old, if not older than Charles, and yet . . ."

"Please." Dallas glanced round. "Let's not discuss Charles, shall we? I'm going for my shower."

"All right." Jane frowned, and then, shrugging, rolled over and closed her eyes. Dallas looked at her for a moment, and then withdrew. She was about to get under the shower when she heard someone knock and enter the chalet.

"Who is it?" she called curiously.

"Me," returned a young voice, and opening the door cautiously, Dallas peered round.

A boy of about eighteen was standing with a tray on which was a teapot, and all the necessary china for afternoon tea. He grinned, and she knew at once that he must be another of Alexander Stavros's brothers.

"I'm Andrea," he said cheerfully. "Shall I leave these here, or would you rather I took them away and came back later with some more?"

"Oh no!" Dallas hesitated. "That is . . . just leave them, I'll see to it all after you've gone."

"I'm sorry I intruded," he replied coolly, not disturbed by her obvious embarrassment. "I did not realise you were bathing. My brother will be most annoyed." But he didn't seem at all worried, and Dallas had to smile too. Andrea was like Nikos, and Nikos she could understand without any difficulty.

"Thank you, anyway," she said, as Jane's bedroom door opened.

"I heard voices . . ." began Jane, and then stopped as though turned to stone. Her cheeks went very white, and Dallas thought she was going to faint. "Who . . . who are you?" she asked faintly, of Andrea.

Andrea's eyes were gently appraising. "I am Andrea Stavros. You must be Jane, am I right?"

"Andrea. Oh, I see. . . ." Jane supported herself against the doorpost, and Dallas wished she had not undressed so prematurely.

"And now, I must go," said Andrea. "I have delayed your sister's bath long enough. I will see you both at dinner this evening. *Adio.*"

After he had gone, Dallas wrapped a towel sarong-wise around her slim body and emerged from the bathroom.

Jane had sank down on to a low chair, and Dallas said quietly:

"I gather he was like Paris."

"Like him!" Jane shook her head in bewilderment. "It was Paris's double."

"I guessed as much," said Dallas, walking across to the table where Andrea had placed the tray. "Here, have some tea. It will make you feel better."

Jane sighed. "However will I be able to get used to living with someone who looks so much like Paris?" she asked wearily.

Dallas shrugged. "Think how hard it must have been for Stavros himself. After all, the resemblance must have struck him just as strongly."

Jane looked at her sister. "I know. I'm sorry. I guess I was just feeling sorry for myself."

Dallas sipped her tea thoughtfully. With every incident that occurred she became more and more convinced that they should never have come.

★   ★   ★

Dallas dressed for dinner at the house that evening with not a little trepidation. From her own calculations she surmised that there would be at least twelve people at the dinner-table, not counting Stephanos, and Myron, too, should he be on the island. This was a formidable number to someone who was completely unused to mixing freely. Dallas had grown used to Charles, and Mrs. Jennings, and they seldom had company.

Eventually she put on a french navy dress, made of broderie anglaise, which had a scooped-out neckline, short sleeves, and a fully flared skirt which seemed absurdly short. Jane had insisted that her clothes be brought a little more up to date if they were to mix with high society and Dallas, in her in-different mood, had reluctantly agreed. But now she was not so sure.

When she emerged from her bedroom it was to find Jane standing by the open french doors, waiting for her. She looked slim and ethereal in white chiffon, both girls having spent money on this kind of attire, which while being attractive, had made rather a hole in their savings. However, as one dress would have to last for many nights, Dallas thought perhaps that the expense had been justified. Both dresses would stand frequent wearing.

Jane looked critically at her sister. "You

look nice," she conceded at last, "but I do wish you wouldn't continually wear your hair up. You look so much more attractive with it down."

Dallas shrugged and lifted the beaded evening bag she had placed on a chair. "I'm not particularly conscious of wanting to look attractive," she said tolerantly. "I admit I don't want to look a mess when there are to be so many critical eyes upon us, but conversely, I see no reason to make any attempt to consider myself attractive. These people are not our people, Jane. I would have thought you would be more conscious of this than I am."

"Why?" Jane faced her sister curiously. "Because of the baby?"

"Of course. Look, Jane, don't start an argument. I don't want to talk about it any more."

Jane grimaced. "Dallas darling, you can't close your eyes and ears while you're here, you know. People are people, no matter how rich or powerful they may seem. They have the same desires and hates, and their bodies require the same satisfactions."

"Am I to understand that you still find this kind of life desirable?"

"Oh, Dallas!" Jane gave an exclamation. "Stop trying to act like an ostrich and bury your head in the sand! You know perfectly well that 'this kind of life' as you call it is infinitely desirable. However, I no longer have any illusions about it, if that's what you mean. I wouldn't be fool enough to behave stupidly a second time. But that doesn't stop me from appreciating the side-benefits."

Dallas walked to the door. "I think we ought to be going," she said. "It's already ten minutes to nine. We don't want to be late."

Jane smiled. "No, that would never do," she agreed, rather mockingly.

As they crossed the grass towards the floodlit forecourt of the villa, she gripped Dallas's arm for a moment, and said:

"I rather think, darling, that you're the one who's going to find life rather complicated here."

Dallas stared at her uncomprehendingly, and Jane's eyes widened.

"Don't you agree? I mean, Alexander Stavros does seem to . . . how shall I put it . . . amuse himself by talking to you and watching the sparks fly. Don't ask me how I know. I can just sense it. The atmosphere between you two is electric!"

"I've never heard anything so ridiculous!" exclaimed Dallas angrily, sure now that Jane was merely taunting her for her own amusement. At times Jane could be very cruel. She was glad when they emerged into the lights, and their intimate conversation ceased.

Nikos came to greet them as they entered the hall and were announced by the white-coated manservant. Resplendent in a white dinner jacket, he smiled benevolently at the two girls, and after complimenting them both on their appearance, he led them into the room, and introduced them to the other guests and members of the family who were standing about in the lounge having drinks before dinner.

The only member of the Stavros family present whom they had not as yet met was Paula Stavros. She was a little older than Nikos, but not yet married, although a magnificent emerald glittered on the third finger of her left hand. She greeted the girls warmly, and Dallas took an immediate liking to her. Tall and slim, her fairness was in vivid contrast to the other members of the family, and Dallas wondered how two such opposites in colouring and looks could be brother and sister.

They were introduced to Paul and Vyria Sharef, and it was during this introduction that Dallas became aware of Alexander Stavros watching her through half-closed lids, while a deliciously voluptuous brunette, Dahlia Sharef, obviously was trying to gain his undivided attention. Tonight, in a dark dinner jacket, with a scarlet cummerbund about his narrow waist, he looked faintly oriental, the line of his beard alienating his appearance entirely. Dallas looked sharply away, but in a moment was forced to acknowledge him again when she was introduced to Dahlia.

Dahlia, in a clinging sheath of black satin, barely glanced at Dallas before continuing to speak caressingly to Alexander Stavros, in their own language.

Dallas became aware that she was alone with Nikos, and looked round for Jane, only to find her with Andrea Stavros, his dark head bent close to her, listening attentively to what she was saying. Dallas, a little disturbed, sighed, and looked up at Nikos thoughtfully.

"You would like another drink?" he asked, indicating the half-empty glass of *ouzo* in her hand.

Dallas shook her head. At his persistence she had accepted the locally popular aperitif, but it was rather more potent than she had thought and she did not want to feel heady, so she refused politely.

Madame Stavros was with Vyria Sharef now, and as their eyes turned in Jane's direction, Dallas wondered what their conversation might be. It was natural that they should find the two girls food for discussion, but Dallas hoped they did not condemn Jane for something that was only half her fault.

A waiter informed them that dinner was served, and they all crossed the wide hall to another long room, set with a polished refectory table that glittered with silver and china, candelabra providing the only illumination. Several centre-pieces of flower-arrangement perfumed the already warm night air, and Dallas thought it was rather fantastic to remember who she was and where she was after the comparative uniformity of their lives. This was like one of those advertisements for high living which she had seen on the television back home, and quite honestly, despite her jumpy nerves and churning stomach, it all seemed quite unreal.

She was seated between Nikos and Jane, with Andrea on Jane's other side. Madame Stavros occupied one end of the table, while

Alexander Stavros himself occupied the other with Dahlia Sharef on his left hand. As Dallas was much farther down the table, towards the opposite end in fact, she felt rather grateful, for it obliterated any necessity to attempt to avoid his gaze, which she was aware lingered on her rather sardonically, as though deliberately trying to infuriate her. She supposed her attitude towards him in England had been less than polite, but there was something about him which made her want to rebel, to fight him every inch of the way. She couldn't understand it, but it was there nevertheless.

The meal was long, and the dishes various, but Dallas's stomach was too disturbed to appreciate such rich and spicy food. The grilled lobster was delicious, but she was not so keen on moussaka, which turned out to be layers of mincemeat and sliced aubergines cooked in a creamy sauce, which was quite tasty but too much for her. The cheese at the end of the meal was excellent, as were the dishes of grapes and figs which other members of the party ate indiscriminately. She tasted *retsina*, the most popular Greek wine, which was a little bitter for her taste. She was greatly relieved when the meal was over, and they could rise from the table and escape to the terrace for some fresh air.

The hall had been cleared, and the younger members of the group had set a record-player going. Several cars roared into the drive about this time, and Nikos said that they were friends of Natalia and Maria. It was only then that Dallas realised that neither Natalia nor Maria had been present for dinner. Yet another hurdle to surmount, thought Dallas dejectedly.

Jane was dancing with Andrea, if it could be called dancing, when Nikos escorted Dallas to the archway which led into the hall. The music was strictly "pop" and Dallas recognised the current top ten quite easily. Jane seemed to be enjoying herself, and she was glad. Surely Natalia would not cause more bother tonight?

She became aware of someone at the other side of her, and she looked up into Alexander Stavros's enigmatic eyes. He was alone, Dahlia Sharef shaken off, and quite relaxed and at his ease.

"You see," he said lightly, "we are not entirely behind the times. We do keep up to date with the current music trends, and I see that Jane is a perfect match for Andrea's gyrating war-dance."

Dallas smiled, and said: "Do you dance, Mr. Stavros?"

"Like that?" he shrugged. "If I had to, I expect I should survive. However, that is not my intention at the moment."

He looked down. "Can you . . . er . . . do the Watusi, or whatever that is meant to be?"

Nikos laughed. "Can you, Dallas?"

Dallas shrugged. "Well, I should be able to. It's not too difficult." She looked recklessly at Nikos. "Shall we try?"

Alexander Stavros's fingers curved round her upper arm. "I think not," he murmured softly. "I want to talk to you. Excuse us, Nikos. This is business, you understand?"

Nikos grimaced, and thrust his hands into his trouser pockets just as Natalia, looking very attractive in a scarlet silk trouser suit, came into the room at the head of a group of young people, boys and girls. She looked round speculatively, her eyes resting on Jane derisively, and then she said:

"I'm sorry. I didn't know our 'guests' would still be here. We skipped dinner deliberately, but it looks as though we're still a little early!"

"Natalia!" Her mother's voice was shocked in the silence.

Alexander Stavros released Dallas's arm, and walked slowly across the floor to where his sister stood, defiantly staring at him.

"Well, Natalia," he said, in a cold, clear voice, "are you such a small person that it is necessary to shout for us all to hear you? Your obvious lack of politeness is of no importance to me; I am used to such displays of childish temperament. Why don't you stamp your feet, or throw a tantrum, like you used to do when you could not get your own way? Or perhaps you would like to have a fight with Jane, as she is apparently your objective in this display of foolishness. Which is it to be? Or would you rather I put you over my knee here and now, and administered the kind of punishment you deserve in front of your friends?"

Natalia's cheeks turned pink, then red, and finally paled to whiteness. She looked up at her brother with trembling lips.

"How can you?" she gasped, her voice breaking. "How can you treat me like this, when it is you for whom I do it?"

"How so?" Stavros's voice was clipped.

"Paris was your *son!*" Natalia's tone was fevered.

"You think you need to remind me of

this?" he snapped angrily. "You think I need your idiotic stupidity to remind me that my son is *dead*!"

"No, Alex. I thought . . ." Her voice trailed away.

"May I remind *you* that this girl you seek to humiliate is at this moment carrying a child which can only be Paris's! Is this anybody's fault? Is it hers? Do you think she wants the child? Then is it Paris's? Who knows? But, Natalia, I want no more of your games, is this understood? I will not have it, do you hear? My involvement in this is as total as yours, more so! So let me be the judge of who is the villain and who the victim!"

His icy tones penetrated every corner of the room. The record-player was for the moment silent, and Dallas felt as though every nerve in her body was stretched to infinity.

Alexander Stavros turned away from Natalia, and then glanced back. "Do not imagine I will forget this episode, Natalia. And do not think you can escape by disappearing again. You will stay, and act naturally. Correct?"

"Yes, Alex." Natalia was subdued, and Dallas was frankly amazed. Only someone she admired tremendously could have quelled

138

Natalia in that mood, and it was obvious she worshipped her eldest brother as her eyes followed him soulfully across the floor.

As though at an unseen signal, the record-player was restarted and the group on the dance floor enlarged considerably. Alexander Stavros made his way back to Dallas's side, and said: "Now, come. I want to speak with you."

Dallas glanced helplessly at Nikos, hoping he would come, too, but he merely smiled encouragingly and told her he would see her later.

Stavros led the way down a panelled corridor to double white doors at the far end which opened into a large comfortable room which seemed to be a study-cum-library, with booklined walls, and deep leather chairs and couches. The colours were all blues and greens with muted shades of yellow in the curtains. Alexander Stavros closed the doors firmly, drew the heavy drapes across the windows and lit several lamps about the room for illumination. It was a very restful atmosphere here, and Dallas felt herself relax almost unconsciously.

He indicated that she should sit on a low green leather couch, and then walked across to a table on which was a tray of drinks of every kind.

"What will you have?" he asked, pouring himself a stiff whisky.

Dallas shook her head. "Nothing, thank you," she declined.

Ignoring her refusal, he poured her a generous measure of brandy and added a little soda, and then crossing to the couch seated himself beside her, his eyes amused as she refused the glass.

"I insist," he said, in a voice soft yet insistent, and with some chagrin she accepted the brandy and sipped it cautiously. It was delicious, though, and she lay back with her drink allowing herself the pleasure of just looking at him. Swallowing most of his drink, he unfastened the top button of his shirt and pulled the knot of his tie loose. Then, his eyes intent upon her, he said:

"I hear from Stephanos that there was some trouble before you left. What was all that about?"

"You know perfectly well what it was all about," retorted Dallas, uneasily aware of his almost primitive physical attraction.

"Tell me," he said insistently, and Dallas compressed her lips and accepted the cigarette he offered her, glad of something to do with her hands. She wondered how he could verbally slay his sister one minute and yet appear so lazily relaxed the next. There was only one solution; he was not relaxed at all, but merely presenting a lazy façade, like a tiger who is just waiting to pounce on its next victim. Unconsciously, she moved slightly away from him along the wide couch, and by so doing drew his attention to her again.

"Well?" he said mockingly. "I'm waiting to hear what happened."

Dallas sighed. "You told Charles that we would be going with you regardless of whether he changed his opinions or not."

"Yes, I admit to that."

Dallas stared at him angrily. "But why? Surely you can see we don't fit in here. Your mother doesn't want us, Natalia isn't even polite; we would have been much better just staying in England. Charles was naturally shocked at first, but that doesn't mean . . ." Her voice trailed away. "What's the use? You never take any notice of our feelings anyway."

Alexander Stavros's eyes narrowed. "Is that so?" he said coolly. "And what might your feelings be? That you would rather stay in

England with that apology for a man called Charles Jennings?"

"You have no right to criticise Charles." Dallas was fuming. "At least he can only love one woman at a time!"

As soon as she said the words Dallas regretted them. Alexander Stavros looked absolutely furious. He drew hard on the cheroot he was holding and then stood up restlessly, as though unable to trust himself so near to her.

"No one speaks to me like that," he bit out, his dark eyes blazing with fire in their depths.

Dallas took a deep breath. "Then perhaps they ought to."

Alexander Stavros studied her deliberately for a few moments, and then he looked away, crossing to the drinks table to pour himself another drink. When he came back he had control of himself again.

"Let it be known," he said icily, "I love no one, no woman, that is, in such a way as to make her indispensable to me. Is that understood? My life is my own to do with as I choose." He smiled sardonically. "However, as you have noticed, I do have a small experience of women, and what I know of them is scarcely appealing. But I would be the first to admit that women have their uses, and I use them."

Dallas's cheeks burned uncomfortably. She would never be able to win an argument with him; his method of attack was wholly devastating. As for his remarks about having a small experience of women, she doubted whether this adjective was sweeping enough. He seemed to know far too much about her sex.

"Why are you telling me this?" she asked, trying to remain calm.

"You started it," he reminded her smoothly.

"Only indirectly. Anyway, what I said is true. We're not wanted here, and there are still several months to go. It will be awful!"

Alexander Stavros swallowed his second drink easily, and then regarded the empty glass in his hand a trifle cynically, Dallas thought.

Then he looked at her, and her pulse quickened uncontrollably. Those dark eyes of his were too piercing.

"I must confess," he murmured, "you interest me as no woman has interested me for a very long time." Dallas pressed a nervous hand to her throat, and he smiled. "I think it is your completely unrealistic attitude," he went on. "After all, you must have ascertained the possibilities available here by now, and yet you still want to leave. I can't quite understand that. Doesn't money interest you at all?"

Dallas ran a tongue over her dry lips. "I . . . I only need money to live," she replied quickly. "Money, as such, as a means to complete wealth and idleness doesn't appeal to me."

"Amazing," he said, shaking his head. "However, there is yet time for you to change your mind. I dare say your sister is less . . . shall we say . . . naïve than you are."

Dallas rose to her feet, unwilling to continue this conversation any longer, but he said, "Sit down, I haven't finished yet. I want to tell you about the occupation I have arranged for you to fill in your time."

Dallas stared at him. "A job!" she exclaimed. "Oh!"

"Aren't you interested now?"

"Of course. It's just I . . . well, I forgot," she finished lamely.

He looked sardonic, and then turned away to the drinks table again. Dallas watched him pour himself another drink and glanced at her own glass. She had hardly finished her first and this would be his third drink. He saw her eyes, and sighed. "I suppose now you think I drink too much," he remarked, an amused expression in his eyes. "Go on, say it. I'm sure you want to."

Dallas shook her head. "It's no concern of mine."

"No, it's not. But I must confess to drinking more these last few minutes than I usually do. Put it down to the exhilaration of your company, Dallas."

It was the first time he had used her name this evening, and as usual she liked the way he said it, with a slightly foreign inflection.

"You're mocking me," she said, bending her head and sipping her own drink.

He shrugged. "Only because you seem to have forgotten how to relax and enjoy life. You have become, how shall I put it, older than your years. Do you not feel this?"

She stiffened. Those were almost the words Jane had used, and hearing them from him, who could not possibly know her as well as Jane disturbed her. Was it so obvious? Did she unconsciously act more like Jane's mother than her sister? It was an unpleasant comparison.

"I expect my life has been singularly more responsible than yours," she retorted irritatedly.

"You think so? When I have the lives of several thousand men in my control?"

"You have managers, directors who can be delegated your duties."

"I suppose I have. Nevertheless, delegation of duty is not one of my vices. I prefer to know a little of what is going on if, as you say, I do not always find it necessary to supervise. Anyway, enough of this. We are digressing. The job I have in mind for you should suit you very well. My brother Paul, who is married and lives further round the coast from here, has two small daughters, Eloise and Estelle. They are six and require tuition before attending a . . . what you would call . . . boarding-school, or academy. Do I make myself clear?"

"Perfectly," Dallas nodded. "Do they really need a governess?"

"Yes, really. Paul's wife, Minerva, has been advocating such a thing for over a year now, but Paul has always said they were too young. You will have gathered they are twins, and quite mischievous in their own way. They speak English, of course. All my family are reasonably well educated in this direction, but now they require more than games; they need reading tuition, and minor teaching in mathematics and writing. Could you handle this?"

"Naturally." Dallas relaxed a little. After teaching a class of over forty eight-year-olds, two six-year-olds did not present many problems.

"Good, then it is settled. Tomorrow I will take you to meet your new charges. It will have to be in the afternoon, as I have plans for the morning which I am unable to break."

Dallas rose to her feet again. "Is that all, then? May I go now?"

He shrugged. "If you want to."

Dallas looked at him awkwardly. "What am I supposed to glean from that remark?" she asked, unable to prevent herself. "Am I free to go, or am I not?"

He half smiled and finished his drink. "I don't know. Maybe it amuses me to talk with you. It's refreshing to find someone who doesn't hang on my every word. You'd never do that, would you, Dallas?"

His voice was deep, and a trifle husky, and Dallas felt a trembling feeling assail her lower limbs. With determined effort she made for the door.

"No," she said, turning the handle, with a strange feeling of reluctance. "No, I wouldn't do that." Then she slipped outside and closed the door behind her.

Only then did she breathe the deep breath she seemed to have been holding for some considerable time. She felt exhausted, both physically and mentally. Verbal sparring with Alexander Stavros might be very stimulating, but it could also be very tiring.

She walked slowly back along the corridor to the hall and came upon Paula Stavros talking to Vyria Sharef. They were seated on a chest, sipping some kind of wine, but Paula rose as Dallas approached, and said:

"Hello, Miss Collins. You are looking tired. Has this day been a very tiring one for you?" She smiled. "Or has my brother been throwing his weight around again?"

Dallas had to smile in return. "Please," she said, "call me Dallas. If you call both of us Miss Collins, we shan't know who you're talking to."

"Very well, Dallas. Naturally you will call me Paula, also." She smiled down at Vyria. "Will you excuse us, Vyria? I want to tell Dallas about the sport here."

Vyria nodded her dark head politely, smiling, although the smile did not quite reach her eyes. Paula slid an arm through Dallas's and drew her across the hall and out on to the terrace overlooking the floodlit swimming pool.

"Sometimes we swim at night," said Paula, indicating the pool. "We used to have bathing parties at one time, but we have not had any recently. Do you swim? Or water-ski?"

"I swim," replied Dallas, "but I've never tried water-skiing. Is it fun?"

"Marvellous fun," exclaimed Paula. "You must learn. My boy-friend Georges is an expert. He will be here later in the week, and he will teach you if I ask him. Would you like that?"

Dallas thought of the contrasting natures of the two Stavros girls she had met. Paula seemed so calm and friendly, while Natalia was all fire and passion. Which of them was most like Alexander Stavros? She had the feeling that despite his controlled exterior, Alexander was more likely to be like Natalia, for there was fire in his eyes, and she was convinced he was not an indifferent lover. Her face turned pink in the shadow of the terrace, and she was glad Paula could not read her thoughts. To imagine Alexander Stavros making love, making love to her, perhaps; to feel those hard brown hands sliding over her flesh, to experience the demanding pressure of his mouth against hers, to be able to slide her arms around his neck; she brought herself up short. Oh, God, she thought, feeling nauseated suddenly, I'm not like that; I don't care about him; I would hate to be another of his *women*!

Paula, completely unaware of Dallas's inner torment, turned to her.

"How about tomorrow?" she said lightly. "After breakfast."

"Tomorrow? After breakfast?" Dallas swallowed hard. "I'm sorry, I was dreaming. What did you suggest?"

Paula laughed. "I thought you might like to have a look around. The house, etc., and the grounds. We might even swim, if you'd like to. Dress casually. No one dresses formally here, during the day, anyway."

"All right, I'd like that," Dallas nodded, glad of anything to banish her unwelcome thoughts.

"Good. I'll call for you after breakfast. By the way, everyone breakfasts in their rooms, usually, except perhaps Alex. So yours will be served in your chalet. O.K.?"

150

Dallas nodded. "It sounds wonderful." She hesitated. "Tell me, your brother says that your twin nieces require a governess; is this so?"

Paula frowned. "Eloise and Estelle? I guess they could at that."

"I . . . I understood from your brother that their mother has advocated one for some time."

"Minerva? Really! Has she? I didn't know that."

Dallas shivered suddenly. "Do . . . do you think it's a good idea, then?"

Paula shrugged. "Why? Are you going to be that person?"

"If . . . if it's acceptable, to all concerned."

"I don't see why not. The twins do run wild. But so did we all at their age. Particularly Alex. He was the wildest of us all."

Dallas bent her head. She couldn't undertand why Alexander Stavros should go out of his way to invent a job for her, when he knew that she had no choice now that she was here, but to accept her position gracefully. Unless he wasn't quite as unfeeling as she believed. She sighed, and as Paula had excused herself again to go and speak to Dahlia Sharef, Dallas walked along the terrace and looked out across the lawns to the sweep of the coastline. Twinkling lights of vessels broke the almost inky darkness. There was no moon tonight, but the air and the perfumes and the whole atmosphere breathed romance. It was easy to feel disturbed in such surroundings, she thought, trying to assimilate her emotions clinically.

But no matter what she told herself she could still picture him sitting beside her on the low couch in his study, his shirt and tie loosened, and she still wanted to touch him.

CHAPTER FIVE

THE next morning Dallas put all such thoughts out of her mind. The translucent quality of the air, and the vista from their chalet windows were enough for the moment to lighten her mood, and she slid out of bed willingly, and showered before breakfast.

But when she went into Jane's room, she found her sister lying in bed looking rather pale and sorry for herself.

"Jane!" she exclaimed. "What's wrong?"

Jane sighed and shook her head, shading her eyes with her arm.

"I feel ghastly," she said. "I think it might have been all that dancing last night. But Andrea was such a marvellous companion, and I didn't like to be a spoilsport."

Dallas frowned. "That's crazy! You're pregnant, Jane. Surely Andrea ought to have had more sense!"

"I guess he's not used to dancing with pregnant women," remarked Jane, with a half chuckle, making an attempt at gaiety. "Oh,

153

Dallas, don't look like that, darling. I'll be okay. It's nothing serious, you know. Just I'm tired, that's all.''

Dallas was less confident, but she agreed to give Jane her breakfast in bed, and they sat having coffee together and eating the delicious rolls and butter, together with the lime marmalade, which Yanni had brought for them earlier.

After the meal was over, Dallas went to get dressed, and decided to wear slim-fitting pale blue pants and a chunky V-necked white sweater. She was combing her hair prior to putting it up when there was a knock at their door.

Closing Jane's bedroom door, Dallas went to open it, and found Andrea on the doorstep.

"Oh," she said, disconcerted. She had expected Paula. "Won't you come in?"

Andrea smiled, his eyes admiring. "You have beautiful hair," he said, disconcerting her even more. "Why do you hide it in that awful bun?"

"It's not a bun!" exclaimed Dallas defensively. "It's a pleat."

"Well, anyway, I like it as it is," Andrea grinned. "Where's Jane?"

Dallas frowned. "Jane is still in bed. She's not very well."

Andrea looked immediately disturbed, and Dallas thought Jane must have made quite an impression on him, one which she had hoped was not returned.

"What is wrong?" he asked fervently. "Is she ill?"

Dallas studied him for a moment. "You *do* know she's pregnant?"

Andrea's cheeks darkened a little. "Yes."

"Well, you ought to know that pregnant girls can't indulge in energetic dancing half the night without feeling some effects."

"Oh lord!" Andrea clapped a hand to his forehead. "How thoughtless of me! I'm very sorry, Dallas. May I . . . may I see her for a moment?"

"I . . . I think not. I also think you ought to tell your brother that a doctor's opinion might not come amiss."

"What?" He frowned. "Oh, I see. You would like the doctor to see Jane."

"Yes," Dallas nodded firmly.

"I will tell him at once." Andrea opened the door again. "I am sorry to have behaved so foolishly."

"It was hardly your fault," replied Dallas, smiling. "And thanks for being so nice."

Andrea hesitated for a moment, looked as

though he was about to say something, and then, smiling, went away. Dallas closed the door, leaned back against it, and wondered whether there were going to be even more problems here than she had even thought possible.

She finished doing her hair, plaiting it and making a coronet on top of her head instead of the usual pleat, as if she went swimming with Paula it would be easier to control in plaits. Then she looked into Jane's room. She seemed to be asleep, so Dallas lit herself a cigarette and opened the chalet door, then went outside on to a kind of patio which fronted the house. It was tiled with coloured tiles, and there was a basket-weave chair, so she sat down and sighed with a feeling of contentment in her surroundings which she had not experienced last night and which she had no reason really to feel this morning. After all, things were just as complicated, and the sensuous sensation of wonder at the view ought not to arouse such inertia inside her.

She felt in her trousers pocket and slid her dark sunglasses on to her nose, for even at this hour—it was a little after nine—the sun was quite brilliant. It was easy to see why so many people took to the lotus-eating life, she thought. It was a pleasant existence to imagine yourself with absolutely nothing to do, and the sun to warm you.

She had been there for about half an hour when she heard voices and looking up saw Paula coming through the trees towards the chalet with an elderly man, carrying a bag.

"Hello, Dallas," said Paula, smiling. "This is Doctor Zantes. Doctor Zantes, this is the patient's sister, Dallas Collins."

The elderly man smiled and shook hands with Dallas, and then they all went inside the building.

"What exactly is the trouble?" asked Doctor Zantes, before they entered Jane's bedroom.

Dallas explained awkwardly, and Paula, sensing her discomfort, said: "Doctor Zantes knows that Jane is pregnant. Alex informed him long before you arrived. Alex is very thorough in his arrangements."

"Oh, I see." Dallas was relieved. "Well, perhaps if you examine her, Doctor, you will be able to tell whether she is all right."

The man smiled. "Of course. Do not worry, Miss Collins. Contrary to regular belief, babies do not abort themselves without a great deal of persuasion."

Dallas nodded, and indicated Jane's room. The doctor went in alone, and Paula turned to Dallas, smiling.

"Are you ready for our date?"

"Well, I am, if Jane is all right." Dallas sounded doubtful.

Paula shrugged. "With Andrea positively yearning to come and keep her company I should think you would be allowed a little freedom," she said.

"Oh, but, I mean . . ." Dallas halted. "It's not the same, is it? I think Jane might want me to . . . Andrea is a man!" she finished lamely.

Paula laughed. "Andrea may be very much like Paris to look at," she said, sobering. "But in other ways he is completely unlike him. For instance, Andrea would never take advantage of any girl. On that I would stake my reputation." As Dallas looked at her anxiously, she went on: "Andrea is more like Alex. Completely reliable."

"*Reliable!*" Dallas could not help but echo the words. Reliable was the last adjective she would have applied to Alexander Stavros. And yet hadn't she once before sensed that feeling of security in his company? Maybe his attitude towards her was tempered by her

158

own treatment of him. And in any case, in family matters, he had shown he was dependable.

"Well, all right," said Dallas slowly. "If the doctor says she is only tired out."

The doctor emerged a few minutes later, closed Jane's door and nodded satisfactorily.

"Over-exertion," he remarked, putting away his stethoscope. "She will be all right if she spends a couple of days in bed, and rests for a couple more. It was the most sensible thing to send for me, although I am afraid your sister did not take too kindly to my presence. I think she wants to see you now." He handed Dallas a bottle of tablets. "Be sure she takes these three times a day and when they are finished advise me and I will let you have some more. They are merely an iron additive. Most women in her condition require added iron."

"Thank you." Dallas took the tablets, and glancing at Paula she went into Jane's room. Jane was propped up on the pillows now, and looked rather annoyed.

"Whatever did you call the doctor for?" she asked, as soon as Dallas had closed the door. "Heavens, I'm okay!"

"You've hardly seen a doctor since you

started this baby," replied Dallas carefully. "It was time you were examined thoroughly. After all, you don't want anything to go wrong, for your own sake, do you?"

Jane grimaced and shrugged. "I suppose not. Oh lord, Dallas, I've got months to go yet. I'm going to be a positive sketch to look at by the time I have it."

"All women look the same," said Dallas comfortingly.

"Yes, and most women are married, with husbands to support them," said Jane bitterly.

"Oh, Jane!" said Dallas, unable to think of anything to say. Then she smiled encouragingly. "Anyway, do you want to see Andrea? He wants to come and keep you company while I . . ."

Jane interrupted her before she could finish. "To keep me company?" she echoed resentfully. "Where are you going?"

Dallas sighed. "If you'd give me a chance I'd tell you," she replied quietly. "Paula wants to show me around, the grounds and so on. It's quite an innocent expedition, and naturally I shouldn't go and leave you alone."

Jane pouted, looking sulky. "Honestly, Dallas, and I'm suppposed to lie here all day and view the sunshine through the window!"

Dallas ran a tongue over her dry lips. "Jane, be reasonable. This afternoon I'm going to see the brother of Mr. Stavros, who has two young children who require tuition. I'm to be their governess, providing their parents approve of me. As such, my hours of freedom will be limited. Surely you don't object to me taking this chance to look around, to explore?"

Jane frowned. "You didn't tell me anything about this."

"I didn't know myself until last night," said Dallas calmly. "Mr. Stavros explained it all to me. I was pleased. After all, my presence here is purely involuntary, I assure you."

Jane studied her fingernails thoughtfully. "What am I supposed to do while you're working?"

Dallas shrugged. "Oh, heavens, Jane, I don't know. Read, knit, sew! After all, you are supposed to be taking it easy; I am not."

"It appears to me that your time here is going to be infinitely more enjoyable than mine," retorted Jane, grimacing. "I wish . . . oh, how I wish I didn't have this . . . this awful encumbrance!"

"Without your so-called encumbrance, neither of us would be here," Dallas reminded her dryly. "Please, Jane, try and accept the situation. I've had to, and it's been more difficult for me, believe me, whatever you may think. I'm not the type to vegetate. That's why I wanted this job. You know perfectly well that with Andrea around you won't be bored."

Jane looked pensive. "I suppose you could be right," she conceded slowly, and then she smiled a little. "All right, we'll play it by ear. But don't blame me if you find yourself getting into emotional difficulties. I think you're crazy separating us like this. We would be much safer together."

"I don't know what you mean," exclaimed Dallas. "How will I get into difficulties teaching two six-year-olds?"

Jane raised her eyebrows mockingly. "Oh, Dallas darling, you won't look beyond your nose, will you? Last night I could have sworn you were bewitched when we found you on the terrace, and yet this morning you act like the actual Norwegian fiord!"

"Oh, Jane!" Dallas turned briskly towards the door. "Anyway, is it all right if I go with Paula?"

"Of course. I'll be fine." Jane was looking rather smug, and Dallas felt unreasonably annoyed with her. She left the room, closing the door with a definite click, and looked up to meet Paula's enquiring eyes.

"Is Jane all right?" asked Paula.

"What? Oh, yes, perfectly all right," said Dallas, a trifle absently, and then gathering her thoughts she said: "Do you want to see her before we go?"

★　★　★

Exploration of Lexandros proved the island to be even more delightful than even Dallas had imagined. There was so much colour and vegetation, with white-sanded coves, sheltered from fresh breezes by rocky headlands providing the coastline with a constantly changing geography. It had a kind of untamed beauty that was hard to describe, but Dallas felt an unfamiliar sense of well-being pervade her whole being, and she felt very glad to be alive on such a wonderful morning.

Paula was driving an open sports car and they followed the road which embraced the island, curving sometimes close to the shoreline so that flurries of sand were scattered in their path, and at others mounting the rocky inclines where gorse and heather flourished wildly, and the air was sweet with the scent of pine.

At the pinnacle of one of these inclines they came upon a small ruined temple and Paula turned the car off the road into the shade of a clump of olive trees.

"I've brought some coffee," she said, sliding out of the car. "We'll have it here. This is the local shrine, you know. It's from this that Lexandros derives its name. Do you like it?"

Dallas climbed out of the car, smoothing back wisps of hair which had come loose during the drive and were curving round her ears. She smiled. "It's quite beautiful, isn't it?" she murmured softly. "Oh, Paula, I'm glad we came here. What is it? Do you know its history?"

Paula laughed, lighting a cigarette before replying. "Do *I* know its history?" she echoed incredulously. "It was practically our catechism when we were children. We heard of Lexa almost as soon as we learnt to talk."

"Lexa?"

164

"Yes. This is the Temple of Lexa. Come on, I'll show you around."

The ruined temple was overhung with wisteria and bougainvillea, and their perfumes enhanced its atmosphere of immortality. It was small, but there were still evidences of its original intent. Ionic columns guarded a marble-floored terrace which led up to a higher level in the centre of which was a stone basin below an altar. Dallas walked forward curiously, followed rather more slowly by Paula who leaned against one of the marble slabs which had formed the walls of the temple but which now gave on to the cliffs above a rocky promontory.

"What is this?" asked Dallas, pointing down into the basin which was now pitted and crumbling a little with age.

Paula smiled. "That was the place where the altar fire burned," she remarked patiently. "It was reputed to burn always; Lexa's fire."

"And who was Lexa?"

"Lexa was a god, or rather so we were taught. A rather lesser-known personage, I would say, but possessing supernatural powers, as did all the best gods."

Dallas looked disappointed. "Oh, don't

joke about it. I'm serious. And I'm interested. Tell me properly."

Paula subdued her amusement. "All right, Dallas, I'm sorry. I can see you are a romantic, and the story is very romantic, if rather sad."

"Go on, then." Dallas was eager.

"Come, let's have some coffee," said Paula, stubbing out her cigarette. "Then I'll tell you."

Dallas shrugged a little regretfully for having to leave the temple, but she followed Paula back to the car and accepted a cup of aromatic Turkish coffee with good grace.

Paula leaned back against the bonnet of the car, and said:

"Now, Lexa was a god, as I have already told you. He was reputedly a very handsome being, and found no difficulty in attracting members of the opposite sex. But unfortunately Lexa had no time for women. He lived here, quite content on his island, living the life of a lotus-eater. The fire in his temple burned brightly, and it was obvious that it would continue to do so, so long as Lexa was happy." She smiled. "Do you want me to go on?"

"Of course." Dallas was enthusiastic.

"So." Paula ran a tongue over her lips. "One day there was a terrible storm over the islands. A caique was wrecked on the rocks below this very point where the temple stood, and the only survivor was a girl. Her name was Helen, and she was ecstatically beautiful. Lexa fell in love for the first and only time in his life. But he was a god, and she was a mortal, and their love was doomed from the outset. Lexa tried everything in his power to make her forget her earthly life and become immortal like himself, but someone else loved Helen, a boy from Sparta, who one day discovered her whereabouts and came to claim her. Lexa was heartbroken, and the fire in his temple died, never to be rekindled."

Dallas sighed, and looked back at the temple. "What happened to Lexa after that?"

Paula shrugged. "There are various legends, too numerous for me to decide which was the truth. In any case, time is pressing. We must get moving again. You can come back here another day and dream to your heart's content. But for the present. . . ."

Dallas smiled. "All right. But it's a pity the story hadn't a happy ending. I like happy endings."

"Like all romantics," remarked Paula tolerantly. "Come on, let's go."

They drove back to the Stavros villa through vineyards which Paula told her had been there for generations. It was growing much hotter now, but the air was still as clear as ever, and every corner produced a view more spectacular than the last.

Paula halted the car near neatly laid-out lawns to one side of the swimming pool. This morning the pool was occupied; Natalia and several of her friends were making full use of it, while Nikos was lying on an air-bed stretched out lazily in the sun. He propped himself up at their arrival, and called:

"I've been looking for you. Where have you been?"

"I've been showing Dallas the island," replied Paula, walking across the lawn to the pool, followed rather more reluctantly by Dallas. "Where are Alex and Dahlia?"

Nikos shrugged his eyes on Dallas. "Who knows? Actually, I believe they have gone skin-diving. I heard Dahlia suggest it to him last evening."

"Oh! And where's Mother?"

"I believe she's gone down to town. She wanted some shellfish for dinner this evening, and naturally she trusts no one else to get it for her."

"Good." Paula seemed pleased. "Dallas and I are just going to see the house."

"Is Dallas interested in the house?" asked Nikos, lying back lazily. "After spending the morning sightseeing with you, I would have thought she might enjoy a swim."

Paula looked at Dallas. "Would you prefer that?"

Dallas struggled to find an answer. Without appearing rude she could hardly give her reasons for not wanting to swim with Natalia.

"I would like to swim," she began cautiously. "But I would also like to see the house. As that was our plan, why don't we follow it?"

Nikos grinned. "Now you're only being diplomatic," he remarked. "Go and put on your swimsuit. Paula, she's going swimming! With me!"

Paula shrugged good-naturedly. "All right. I guess you can see the house any time. I think I'll have a shower before lunch."

Left with Nikos, Dallas wished she had been more firm and insisted on seeing the villa with Paula. But now she was committed,

169

so she might as well make the best of it. The group of young people at the other end of the pool were eyeing her curiously, and she felt sure Natalia would say something.

But she didn't, and after a moment they continued with their antics as though unaware of her existence.

"Go and get changed," said Nikos, propping himself up again. "You have brought a swimsuit, I suppose?"

"Of course." Dallas glanced around. "What time is it, anyway? I've left Jane for long enough already really."

Nikos glanced at his watch. "It's noon," he replied. "Lunch isn't for hours yet. And Andrea is with Jane. He's taken the record-player and the records, so I don't suppose they'll be missing you."

"Well, anyway, I shall have to go back to the chalet to change."

"Don't be long," said Nikos, relaxing again, and shrugging her slim shoulders Dallas walked away.

She walked round the side of the villa where the trees grew thickly and close to the house. She looked down on to the beach and saw the breakers on the sand, and breathed deeply. She did not see the man coming from the opposite direction until she had practically touched him.

"Oh!" she exclaimed in surprise, looking up into Alexander Stavros's dark features. "I'm sorry, I wasn't thinking what I was doing." She noticed he was carrying goggles and flippers, and a pair of oxygen cylinders. Obviously Nikos had been right; he had been skin-diving. With Dahlia? Dallas wondered. It would be very nice, she thought, to explore the undersea world in company with someone who was probably an expert.

"You were dreaming, perhaps?" he asked now. "Has our island begun to enchant you in spite of yourself?"

"I like it, who wouldn't?" she said shortly. "If that's what you mean."

He smiled, rather sardonically she thought, and then said:

"I will expect you to be ready at four o'clock for our trip to my brother's home. I shall not be lunching at home, but I will be back for you then."

"All right," Dallas nodded, unable to prevent a surge of excitement start within her at the prospect of the afternoon ahead. Alexander Stavros nodded, and continued on his way, and Dallas made her own way to the chalet.

The door to Jane's bedroom stood wide, and there was the sound of rhythmic music from the record-player. Andrea was seated on Jane's bed and they were examining some colour slides which were in a plastic container. When Dallas looked into the room, Jane looked up and her face had lost its earlier sulkiness.

"Do you know, Dallas," she cried, "Andrea has a ciné camera and he's going to take a film of me as soon as I'm able to get up. Isn't that marvellous?"

"Marvellous," agreed Dallas, relieved to find Jane in such good spirits. "I'm going swimming. Is that all right?"

"Of course," said Andrea, without giving Jane time to reply. "We're perfectly happy here. While you're out this afternoon, I shall bring some films over I have taken of the family from time to time, and give Jane a film show, yes?"

Jane was enthusiastic, and Dallas felt herself relax even more. She thanked the gods for Andrea, and his understanding. At least he was making things easier for Jane, and indirectly for herself.

The swim with Nikos was uneventful, except that he seemed to find her wholly fascinating, and hardly took his eyes off her. And as Dallas was only dressed in a one-piece lemon bathing suit, she felt rather uncomfortable out of the water. Natalia and her friends had left the pool, and were stretched out on the mosaic tiling at the far side of the pool, drinking tall glasses of aperitifs and laughing and talking among themselves.

Lunch was at two, but Dallas rang the house and asked if she could have lunch at the chalet with Jane. She knew this would cause no annoyance. Mrs. Stavros would be only too glad to have her out of the house.

Later, she showered and changed, ready for her trip with Alexander Stavros. Before Andrea arrived to keep Jane company, Jane said:

"I notice you seem to have taken my advice about your clothes, anyway."

Dallas frowned, wondering whether Jane was about to start another argument. "How do you mean?" she asked lightly.

"Simply that you're wearing your skirts shorter, and you seem to be acting less like the maternal protector. I'm not sure I really like it!"

Dallas was nonplussed. "Honestly, Jane," she exclaimed, "you seem determined to undermine my confidence, such little as I have, that is. Maybe you imagine this place is going to my head after all."

Jane shrugged, and reached for a glass of lime juice from her bedside table. "Well, I must admit I didn't expect you to spend our time here going out without me!" She had resumed her resentful manner, and Dallas sighed.

"Jane, please, try and be reasonable. If I have a job, surely that's all to the good! We can't live here on charity, you know. Even if we are provided with free accommodation there are lots of other small things we'll have to pay for; like make-up, toilet accessories, not to mention clothes!"

Jane grimaced, screwing up her nose. "We aren't broke."

"Almost," retorted Dallas. "After the last few weeks of extravagant spending, we aren't exactly affluent."

"You're always worrying about something," said Jane, sniffing. "Heavens, if you asked Alexander Stavros he would give you any amount of money you cared to name!"

Dallas stared at her sister disbelievingly. "You don't seriously imagine I would ever do that, do you?" she cried, in amazement.

"Why not? If the apple's there for the taking, why not take it? I'm having enough to put up with, aren't I?"

Jane in this mood was completely unreasonable, and Dallas turned away, feeling slightly sick. She was beginning to realise that Jane, as a person, was almost unknown to her. She had thought she knew everything about her sister, but it was obvious she had been fooling herself. What was it Alexander Stavros had said? Something about Jane being less "naïve" than herself. Had he, with the shrewdness she herself had witnessed, summed Jane up more honestly? Dallas shook her head a little wearily. Every time she thought they were getting a little out of the wood, back they plunged into its depths with Jane's attitude.

She smoothed the skirt of the lime green cotton suit she was wearing, and walked to the door. "Andrea will be here soon," she said quietly. "I'll see whether the car is waiting for me."

The chalet door stood wide, and as she approached it a shadow blocked the sunlight and Alexander Stavros came to lean lazily against the doorpost. Dressed in a light grey lounge suit, the narrow trousers accentuating the length and strength of the muscles of his legs, he was dangerously attractive, and Dallas felt her stomach turn right over.

"Ready?" he asked, his voice husky, and when she nodded, he said: "How is the invalid?"

"Won't you come in and see for yourself?" said Dallas awkwardly, standing aside so that he could do so. Shrugging, he walked through the door, immediately dwarfing the generous proportions of the room. He entered Jane's bedroom casually, almost as though he was used to entering a woman's bedroom, Dallas thought, and then squashed the idea as she recalled that he had indeed been married, and had known what it was like to see a woman in bed frequently. She wondered what Anna Stavros had been like. She wondered whether Alexander Stavros had been terribly upset at the time of her death. It was likely, she supposed. After all, he was a passionate man, his quick temper proved that, and if he loved someone there would be no half measures. Was that why he had told her that there was no woman now who was indispensable to him? Had all his feelings died with Anna?

To her annoyance, the thought disturbed her not a little. She didn't know why, but the thought of some woman living constantly with Alexander Stavros, sharing his life, his home, his *bed*; again she had to force her brain to reject these thoughts. She didn't know what was the matter with her, thinking like that. She had never had ideas about a man like this before. It had got to stop!

"So? What is troubling you?" Stavros's deep voice close to her ear caused her to start guiltily, and a tell-tale flush coloured her cheeks.

"N . . . nothing," she stammered.

"I should say that was a lie," he remarked casually, walking towards the door. "The way you were gnawing at your lip I would guess that your thoughts were disturbing you considerably."

"You know nothing about it," replied Dallas childishly, and went to say goodbye to Jane. Jane looked at her strangely. She must have overheard their conversation, and her eyes were narrowed frowningly. But she said nothing in particular, and Dallas was almost glad to leave the chalet.

The car Alexander Stavros drove was a white Mercedes tourer, and he helped Dallas in before walking round the bonnet and sliding in beside her.

"Cheer up," he remarked mockingly. "You might *just* enjoy yourself."

Dallas had to smile at this, and she relaxed a little.

"That's better," he said, starting the engine. "We have all afternoon together, and I don't like reluctant passengers."

As the car turned out of the drive on to the road, Dallas glanced back and saw the Sharefs and their daughter walking along the path near the pool. She wondered whether Dahlia objected to his leaving her for the afternoon, but dared not voice such a suggestion at the moment.

The sun was hot, and Dallas slid her dark sunglasses on to her nose. Stavros had put on dark glasses himself when he took the wheel and they successfully disguised what expression she might have perceived in his dark eyes. But for the present she was content just to look at the day, and forget for a while the circumstances of her surroundings. Lunch had been a delicious meal, with prawns, served in oil and lemon sauce, and a sweet confection of Turkish pastries, filled with honey and nuts. Yanni had told them that most of his race observed the continental tradition of the *siesta*, but although Jane had been resting Dallas had been too excited to relax.

The road to Paul Stavros's villa took them back through the village of Lexa, nestling on the curve of the bay, its small harbour just beginning to come to life again. There were numerous caiques and small fishing boats drawn up to the quay, while in the bay a white sailed sloop drifted lazily. It was all very picturesque. And Dallas glanced at her companion as he swerved to avoid a mule laden with baskets of fruit.

"You went out with Paula this morning," he observed, the wheel sliding effortlessly through his lean brown hands. "Where did she take you?"

"We drove quite a way round the island, and she showed me the ruined temple of Lexa."

"Naturally," he remarked lazily. "The local landmark, in fact. What did you think of it?"

"I think it's beautiful," Dallas confessed candidly. "I think the fact that it's overgrown adds to its enchantment."

"Indeed?" He sounded amused now, and

she wished she had not sounded so enthralled.

"Tell me," she said, changing the subject. "You rarely speak any Greek to me. Does it not trouble you to speak English all the time?"

Alexander Stavros smiled. "Not particularly. I was educated in England when I was old enough. I attended Cambridge University and gained a degree in economics. But if you would like me to speak Greek to you, I am quite prepared to do so. The question is, will you understand me?"

Dallas flushed. "I don't speak Greek at all," she said stiffly.

"Well, don't get upset about it," he murmured softly. "I'll teach you a little." He glanced at her thoughtfully. "Now, what would be a useful thing for you to be able to say?" He seemed preoccupied for a moment, and then he said: "Of course: *Chero poli. Onomazo me* Dallas."

"What does that mean?" Dallas was curious in spite of herself.

"Something very simple. 'How do you do, or pleased to meet you, my name is Dallas.' Right?"

Dallas repeated it slowly, and then looked

questioningly at him. "How do I know you're telling me the truth? You might be making me say something terrible."

He laughed, and Dallas bent her head to avoid his mocking eyes. As usual she seemed to find herself at a disadvantage.

"I wouldn't do that," he replied easily. "You seem to have the knack of doing that for yourself."

Dallas compressed her lips and looked away from him, determinedly taking an intensive interest in the scenery again.

Paul Stavros's villa was similar to the family house except that it was smaller, and more compact, and had no pool. Alexander brought the car to a smooth halt at the foot of shallow steps leading up to the main entrance, and Dallas slid out before he had time to walk round to assist her. The sound of the car had aroused someone, for two little girls came running towards them from the direction of the garden, their chubby faces streaked with dirt.

They flung themselves unreservedly on Alexander, and Dallas noticed that he didn't seem to care that their hands were dirty and might mark the immaculate grey suit. Instead, he went down on his haunches beside them and listened intently as they chattered to him in their own language, obviously telling him everything they had been doing since they had seen him last. Dallas had never seen him with children, and she realised with a strange pang that the little girls adored him, and he was completely at his ease with them. Eventually he stood up, and said:

"Come, Eloise, Estelle, we are neglecting your visitor, Miss Collins. She has come to meet you, and if you get along together, she will come back and teach you some useful English lessons. But she does not speak Greek, so we must always speak English in her presence, yes?"

"*Chero poli*, Eloise, Estelle," said Dallas cautiously, allowing the words to slide slowly and carefully off her tongue.

The little girls laughed. They were very pretty, and very dark, but very chubby. Puppy fat, thought Dallas, thinking them adorable.

"But Miss Collins does speak our language," one of them exclaimed, and Alexander smiled, and shook his head.

"Only a few words. What I said before still stands. We will speak English. Now, is your mother at home?"

"Yes, but Papa is away," said the other little girl.

"I know. I saw him this morning," replied Alexander, taking Dallas's arm quite naturally, but causing an electric shock to run up her veins like wildfire. "Come, we will find your mama."

Minerva Stavros was nothing at all like Dallas's nervous expectations. After her experiences with the other members of the Stavros family, except Paula, that is, she had half expected a second Madame Stavros, but she couldn't have been more wrong. Minerva was small, much smaller than Dallas, with curly brown hair, blue eyes, and a piquantly attractive face. She was plump, like her daughters, and in shorts and a sleeveless sweater, fresh from gardening like her children, she was relaxed and approachable and very human. She greeted Dallas warmly and announced that they would have English tea in her honour, and went away to get changed, taking the girls with her.

"Well," said Alexander Stavros, looking at Dallas questioningly, "do you feel less tense now?"

They were in the low light lounge of the villa; Dallas was sitting comfortably on a low chair, while Alexander Stavros leaned lazily against the screened-fire mantelpiece.

"Yes, I do," she said, accepting a cigarette which he leaned forward to offer her, lighting himself the usual cheroot. "She's nice, and somehow *ordinary*, if that won't be taken amiss."

"Of course not. You can be assured I am not a gossip!"

Dallas drew on her cigarette, thinking how strange it was that their lives should have become so closely entangled. Was it only about six weeks ago that she had met him for the first time? Maybe a little more than that, but a short period nevertheless. And so much had happened in that time.

"I am going away tomorrow," he remarked suddenly, tapping ash from his cheroot into the hearth. "I have business in Athens. I will be away about two weeks. The Sharefs are leaving with me."

Dallas felt slightly sick, and stubbed out her cigarette hastily, and with a nervous, jerky movement. "Are you?" she said, her voice assumedly light. "Wh . . . when will I begin my work?"

"As soon as you like. Minerva and Paul are quite agreeable. You can begin tomorrow if

184

you wish. Simeon, one of the servants, acts as chauffeur when required. I will see that a car is put at your service. Materials, books, etc. have all been provided, and are available here. I further believe Minerva has assigned a room in which you, and the girls, may work."

Dallas looked up at him anxiously. "I can't help but feel that your brother and his wife have practically had me forced upon them. Paula knew nothing about them wanting a governess when I asked her."

"Didn't she?" Alexander smiled sardonically. "Well, contrary to your opinion, Paula does not know everything. And Minerva and Paul need a governess for the girls. Need I say more?"

Dallas shrugged. "I suppose not."

"Then cheer up, for God's sake," he muttered, surprising her still more. "You'd think I was asking you to enter the arena with the lions, instead of offering you pleasant employment in pleasant surroundings."

Dallas stiffened, but then Minerva was back, and there was no time to say more. Minerva had changed into slacks and another sweater, and obviously cared little for her appearance. The girls were scrubbed and neat, in print dresses and ankle socks, but they were Minerva's children, and could not be mistaken.

They had tea, although Dallas didn't particularly care for it, and she accepted one of the sweetmeats that Minerva pressed upon her. They discussed the arrangements, and it was agreed that Dallas should come mornings to teach the girls from nine until twelve. It was going to be a very simple occupation for her and Dallas still felt guilty about the whole thing.

She said as much to Alexander Stavros again, on the journey home, and shivered when he got angry with her.

"Why is it you doubt everything I do?" he asked violently. "You doubt my integrity, my responsibilities, and my motives. Why? What have *I* ever done to deserve this kind of treatment from you?"

Dallas bit her lip. "I can't help it," she said, bending her head. "It's probably because I've seen you in various situations that . . . well, that can be misconstrued. Or maybe that's the wrong description. Maybe the life you lead is as careless as it seems."

She looked up and realised that they were not going home the same way as they had come.

"I'd like to know how you have come to this conclusion," he remarked coldly. "What kind of 'situations' are you talking about?"

Dallas hunched her shoulders. "You know perfectly well. In London there was Athene Siametrou, and here there is Dahlia Sharef. It's obvious that you attract the opposite sex, isn't it?"

"Is that my fault?" he asked icily.

"No, not exactly. But you said yourself, you *use* women. That's hardly the kind of remark to arouse compassion in its listener."

"My God! Dallas Collins, you amaze me," he muttered, shaking his head. "What business is it of yours what I do?"

"None."

"Good! I'm glad you understand that." He lit himself another cheroot, and for a while there was silence.

The shadows were lengthening, the afternoon was passing into early evening. Dallas judged the time to be around six-thirty.

They were climbing an incline now, and at the top she recognised the little temple which she and Paula had visited that morning. To her surprise Alexander pulled the car off the road, and halted beneath the grove of olive trees. Then he looked

TLOL 7

187

thoughtfully at Dallas, and slid out of the car.

Dallas felt herself shaking a little, but when he glanced back at her and said: "Come here," she slid reluctantly out of the vehicle.

The grass was soft underfoot, and the scent of mimosa was wild and sweet. Alexander Stavros entered the arched entrance to the temple, stepping over the mossy marble slabs lazily. Dallas followed him, wondering why he had brought her here. The others would be expecting them back, and no doubt Jane would be beginning to feel resentful of her absence. Besides, they had nothing more to say to one another, and Alexander Stavros had made it perfectly plain that he found her attitude annoying.

He had stopped now, and she halted beside him. He was looking down at the basin which had once held the legendary fire of Lexa. "Did Paula tell you what this was?" he asked softly.

In the dusk his features were darkly, arrogantly foreign, and Dallas trembled a little. He smiled, his even teeth very white against the tan of his skin.

"Y . . . yes, she told me," stammered

Dallas awkwardly. "Mr. Stavros, I really think we ought to be getting back."

He studied her features intently, and startled her by running the back of his fingers down the side of her cheek. "You're a very nervous creature tonight, Dallas," he murmured lazily. "What has happened to that determined young woman who spars with me quite unyieldingly?"

Dallas shivered. "I want to go back," she said placidly, marvelling at the calmness of her tone.

"There's no hurry," he replied quietly, the smile still lurking in his eyes.

Dallas turned abruptly away. "Wh . . . what's that noise?" she asked hastily, trying to lighten the tension.

"You call them crickets," he murmured easily. "Didn't you notice them last night?"

"I . . . I must have been too tired," said Dallas, swallowing hard. "What time do you leave in the morning?" Her sentences were forced and jerky, and she knew with his expert knowledge of women he would not find it difficult to sense her discomfort, when he himself was the direct cause of it.

"Forget me for the moment," he answered, running exploratory fingers round the rim of the fire-basin. "Why are you so scared suddenly? What do you expect to happen to you?"

In this remote yet strangely gentle place, Dallas found it difficult to hold on to reality. There was something entirely unreal about this whole incident, and she felt sure that Alexander Stavros had known about the atmosphere of this temple when he brought her here at dusk. The wind through the delicately curved arches which had stood for thousands of years whispered like music, and the crickets added their own rhythm to the sounds of the encroaching night.

She looked round at him, and found his eyes on her disturbingly. "Why have you brought me here?" she asked breathlessly.

He shrugged his broad shoulders. "Maybe to see whether you were as immune from atmosphere as you normally appear to be." He smiled. "And of course you are not. You know that this place has a sense of presence, of immortality, if you like. It shakes off the petty restrictions of earthly life, and gives one a taste of eternity."

Inwardly, Dallas knew he was right. He had voiced her own feelings entirely, but she shook her head, and moved with stumbling steps across the uneven slabs of the lower terrace. She sensed rather than felt him close beside her as she halted uncertainly, looking down on the rocks below the temple.

"Did Paula tell you the end of the legend?" he asked, in her ear.

Dallas shook her head, not trusting herself to speak.

"There are many, of course, but the most popular one is that Lexa threw himself off this cliff on to the rocks below, and because he was a god his spirit sank below the waves, and became a constant warning to sailors, not to come too close to these rocks. Don't ask me how, or why, but there has never been a wreck here since." He gave a short laugh. "It is not a spot frequented by the local population after dark."

Dallas looked up at him, and his eyes darkened, his lids shading the expression in their depths. Her legs turned to jelly, and she shivered involuntarily.

"So," he murmured, drawing her towards him unresistingly. "Now I am the god in charge of the island, are you going to rekindle my fire?"

"Alexander," his name came easily to her lips. "Please, don't!" The appeal in her voice was lost to him, as the warmth of her body penetrated the thin suit he was wearing.

"Don't say that," he murmured achingly, his mouth caressing the side of her neck. "Oh God, you do something to me!"

Then his mouth found hers, and her lips responded involuntarily. Her arms slid round his neck, and the music in the arches became a crescendo in her ears. She was drowning in feeling, sensual feeling, and she lost all sense of time and circumstance. It would have been so easy to succumb to him; she had never known she could respond in such a manner to the touch of a man's hands, while her lips clung to his, willing to go on being hungrily possessed.

But the desire to be possessed and the actual meaning of possession were two entirely different things, and Dallas drew her arms from around his neck, and began pressing him away from her violently, struggling to be free. For a moment he resisted her feeble attempts to escape, and then he let her go, and she stood back quickly, and without looking back pushed her way through the arched portico, across the rich turf to the sanctuary of the car. She badly wanted to cry now, and she wished desperately that she did not have to get into the automobile and wait for him to come to drive her back to the villa.

It was some minutes before he joined her, but when he did so she saw that he was completely composed, and immediately she felt uncomfortable. Looking down at her hands in her lap, she saw that a button of her jacket was loose, and she hastily fastened it, wondering how he could appear so immaculate while she felt hot and untidy, and when he slid into the car beside her, she moved as far away from him as she could along the bench seat.

He glanced her way rather sardonically, and shrugging inserted his key in the ignition. "Relax," he said, his voice cold as a mountain stream. "I don't want to touch you."

Dallas rubbed her cheeks with trembling fingers. The dark beard along his jawline had chafed her a little, and her skin felt tender. Alexander turned the car on to the road again, and then said:

"What's wrong? Apart from your morals digging you, of course!"

Dallas clenched her fists. "Don't speak to me like that!" she said angrily. "My morals are not in question!"

"And mine are?"

"You said it, not me." Dallas stared unseeingly out of the side of the car. "And my cheeks hurt, that's all! You weren't exactly gentle!"

He uttered an angry expletive in his own language. "You didn't exactly object!" he muttered sarcastically.

Dallas's cheeks burned now with embarrassment. "All right, don't let us have an inquest. I ought to have known . . ."

"Damn you, you know absolutely nothing," he ground out furiously. "Not about men in general, and this man in particular! You haven't the faintest idea of the precariousness of your position. Don't ride me, Dallas, or you may find you have bitten off a little more than you can digest!"

"Chew," said Dallas automatically, and then pressed the knuckles of one hand to her teeth, and wished she could dissolve into thin air.

Alexander merely moved his shoulders carelessly, and pressing his foot on the accelerator deliberately sent the powerful car surging hard down the road.

She had not thought that the sight of the Stavros villa would ever seem like home, but it did, when the car halted she slid out without waiting for any further comments from him, and sped across the grass through the trees to the chalet, and Jane.

CHAPTER SIX

THE next morning Dallas prepared for the new job with mixed feelings. It had been relayed to her through the medium of Nikos that Alexander Stavros had left instructions that she should be ready at eight-thirty when Simeon would drive her to Paul Stavros's villa for lessons with Eloise and Estelle. This had been revealed at dinner last evening which she had taken at the house, despite her misgivings, at Nikos's insistence. To her relief Alexander was not present, and in consequence her nerves were less taut.

So today she dressed in a slim fitting shift of blue linen, with a white cardigan about her shoulder, in case she needed it. Before leaving she went into Jane's room. She was looking disgruntled again, and Dallas said quickly: "What's wrong?"

Jane grimaced. "Andrea won't be coming today. His mother had found some unexpected occupation for him. I suspect because she thinks we're becoming too friendly. Isn't it sickening?"

Dallas bit her lip. "Well, you've brought plenty of magazines, surely you can entertain yourself for a couple of hours. I shall be back soon after twelve myself."

"I suppose I can, but I shall be glad when I can get up and about again. I'm not used to such enforced inactivity."

"Of course you're not," agreed Dallas, nodding. "Never mind, you can get up tomorrow, so long as you take it easy."

"I don't want to take it easy," muttered Jane mutinously. "Why should I? I don't want this baby anyway!"

"Oh, Jane, please!" Dallas sighed. "There's nothing either of us can do about that, is there, so stop feeling sorry for yourself!"

Jane was aghast; Dallas had never spoken to her like that before. She hunched her shoulders. "Well, anyway, how did you get on with Alexander Stavros yesterday?" she countered, knowing that Dallas preferred not to discuss their host.

Dallas turned away to hide her expression. "Oh, all right," she replied lightly.

Jane's eyes narrowed. "Did you? How nice! You didn't have much to say about it last night. Come to think of it, you didn't have much to say about anything, did you? Why?"

"Must there be a reason?" asked Dallas wearily.

Jane stared at her sister's back intently. "Usually there is with you. What happened? Did he make a pass at you?"

Dallas clenched her fists. "Oh, don't be so ridiculous!" she exclaimed angrily, and marched out of the room, before she lost her temper altogether. She found she was trembling again, and gripped her handbag tightly. Calm down, calm down, she told herself furiously. *Calm down!*

The ride out to Paul Stavros's house was accomplished in a much shorter time than she and Alexander Stavros had taken the day before, and she could only assume that they had taken a less direct route. Minerva Stavros was there to greet her, and with her was a tall, broad Greek, who vaguely resembled Alexander, except that his features were heavier, and his lips fuller. There was something about him that Dallas didn't particularly like, but as liking her employer was no part of her employment she smiled politely when he was introduced by his wife.

Eloise and Estelle came running down the stairs as they all entered the cool hallway.

The girls were dressed in shorts and sweaters again, and Dallas thought they looked adorable. Paul Stavros excused himself on the grounds that he had business to attend to, and Minerva showed Dallas the schoolroom.

"You'll have complete freedom here," she said, smiling in a friendly fashion. "Eloise and Estelle are good children, and shouldn't cause you too much bother. They are eager and willing to learn, as Alexander has promised they shall attend an English boarding school if they work hard." It was apparent that Alexander Stavros's word held weight among his family.

"Thank you," Dallas smiled. "I only hope they like me."

Minerva smiled conspiratorially. "I'm sure they will. Besides, Alex wouldn't have recommended you without good reason."

Dallas flushed. That man again! Was she never to feel free of him?

In actual fact the children were pathetically eager to please. They listened carefully to everything she said, and worked hard and conscientiously. In fact, during the course of the morning, Dallas began to wonder whether such diligence in ones so young was a good thing. Most six-year-olds were mischievous to a certain extent, but these Stavros children showed no such tendencies. But again, she felt it was not her place to voice opinions, so she accepted the situation, and tried to draw the children out in other ways.

"Tell me," she said, "do you have any brothers or sisters?"

Estelle wrinkled her nose. "No, Miss Collins."

Dallas looked thoughtful. "Do you have many playmates, then?"

"We are not encouraged to mix with the village children," said Eloise sedately. "Daddy says we must entertain ourselves, as there are two of us."

That explained why they were so eager to attend a boarding-school, thought Dallas wryly. With only themselves to play with, even in these idyllic surroundings, they must get bored stiff. She decided to mix a little play with work in future weeks. She might even take them down to the village herself, and explore the tiny harbour.

When she returned to the chalet before lunch she found Jane sunbathing on the patio. She looked up at Dallas's arrival, and said:

"Well? How did it go?"

"Very well," replied Dallas carefully. "Have you been all right?"

"So-so," replied Jane, screwing up her face. "I had a visit from Madame Stavros."

"You did what?" Dallas stared at her sister.

"Yes. Madame herself."

"What did she want?"

"This and that." Jane struggled into a sitting position.

Dallas compressed her lips. "Anyway, what are you doing out of bed? The doctor said you should stay there two days."

"Rubbish!" Jane grimaced. "I feel fine. I'm not lying there like some invalid. In any case, Madame Stavros didn't object when she found me here, and I've no doubt she found out what the doctor had to say."

Dallas sighed. "I can't understand why she should come to see you. Unless it was a purely friendly visit."

"I'd hardly call it that!" remarked Jane annoyingly. "She told me that Andrea would be working the rest of the week, and that he had been neglecting his duties spending so much time with me. Besides, Andrea was an impressionable youth, and ought not to be taken seriously."

Dallas clenched her fists. "Oh, Jane!"

"Yes. So I'm to have a very exciting time. Paula called. She's taking me for a drive this afternoon, so I guess I shall have to content myself with charming the *peasants*!"

Dallas sighed, "Don't take this to heart, Jane."

Jane shrugged. "I won't. It's hardening me up a bit, though. I can't help that. Did you know Alexander Stavros left this morning?"

"I knew he was going, yes," said Dallas cautiously.

"Well, he's gone. And Nikos has gone with him. So you're deserted too. We'll have to comfort one another."

Dallas half smiled. "Perhaps it's just as well," she murmured, and walked into the chalet slowly.

As she showered before lunch she came to a decision. She and Jane would continue to live in the chalet, but in future they would not go over to the house for meals. They could manage perfectly well on their own, and then no one need concern themselves on their behalf. After all, neither Madame Stavros or Natalia appeared to want them there, so they would not be missed, and as Nikos was away it was a golden opportunity to create a precedent. It might be cowardly, she thought, but it might save a little of their self-respect. She refused to consider what Alexander might say on his return.

Thoughts of Alexander she had firmly banished from her mind all day, and last night exhaustion had claimed her in sleep before her mind could begin working its own destruction. But now, in the shower, she allowed herself to remember every second of their last meeting with a kind of tortured anguish. There was so much to remember, and her face grew hot as she recalled the way he had held her in his arms and kissed her, if that savage attack on her emotions could only be called "kissing." She shivered, in spite of the heat; she had known he would make love expertly, just as he did everything else.

The meal arrangements were accepted without question by everyone except Paula, who told Dallas that Alexander would be furious when he found out.

"You're doing exactly as my mother wants," she said hotly. "She is letting her stupid dignity overcome her natural politeness. I'm sorry."

Dallas smiled. "Don't worry, Paula. We would rather avoid too much contact with the family. It causes less friction this way, really it does."

Paula made a helpless gesture, and gave up. She could not force the girls to do as she wanted.

Dallas got to know Minerva Stavros quite well in the days that followed. As her husband was away a lot, a fact that Dallas noted with pleasure, she turned to the younger girl for companionship, and Dallas listened to her confidences with mixed feelings. Without being aware of it, Minerva was involving her ever more deeply in the affairs of the Stavros family. When Paul Stavros was around, Minerva was tongue-tied and awkward, and Dallas didn't like the way Paul tried to catch her eyes with his whenever they were alone together. She thought he was trying to be flirtatious, and she didn't like it at all.

Paula was a frequent visitor to the chalet, and despite his mother's attitude, Andrea came too, whenever he could. This pleased Jane, so Dallas could not object. She supposed her sister was having rather a difficult time, all things considered.

Paula took Dallas and Jane all over the island, and one evening when Andrea was keeping Jane company they went down to the *taverna* in the village.

They seated themselves outside, at one of the pretty tables with umbrella awnings, and Paula ordered Santa Helena, a light wine that Dallas found quite enjoyable. After they had both lit cigarettes, Paula said:

"Truthfully, Dallas, how well do you know Alex now?"

Dallas felt the hot colour surge into her cheeks. "Well, I . . . I guess I know him like any employee knows an employer."

Paula didn't notice her flushed cheeks. "Yes. Do you like him?"

"Oh, I haven't really thought about it," Dallas prevaricated.

Paula nodded. "I suppose it's not the sort of thing you would do," she said thoughtfully. "A lot of women would have taken the opportunity to try to get to know him better. I think he gets sick of cloying females."

Dallas did not reply, not knowing quite what to say.

Paula drew deeply on her cigarette. "Alex has not been particularly happy since his disastrous marriage," she said, surprisingly.

Dallas looked up. "*Disastrous* marriage?" she repeated.

"Of course," Paula frowned. "Naturally, you wouldn't know anything about that."

"I . . . I understood that Mr. Stavros's wife died of leukaemia."

"So she did. After being terribly ill for about seven months. But before her illness, Anna lived quite a different kind of life. Oh, I know she's dead, and one shouldn't speak ill of the dead, but honestly, Dallas, she was a . . . a . . . pig!"

Dallas looked out across the rippling waves of the harbour. "I don't think you ought to talk to me about this," she murmured softly.

"Why? It's no secret. Anna liked men, it's as simple as that. She badly wanted Alex, so she tricked him into marriage, despite the fact that he was already engaged to another girl, and had been so for several years. When he found out he had been tricked he was furious, as any man would have been in the same circumstances, particularly as his feelings towards Anna had been the usual fleeting passion of a man for a beautiful woman. A woman, moreover, who threw herself at his head. He had no real love for her, but for the sake of the family he stayed with her. After two years, when Paris was only a baby, she wanted to leave the island, to go and live in

Athens. He refused, so she went alone, and you can guess what happened." Paula twisted her nose. "It was disgusting! Not that Alex seemed to care particularly. He just buried himself in his work, and if any woman came along I guess he treated them exactly as they would wish to be treated. Later, when Anna got bored, she came back to the island. Minerva Yannides and my brother Paul had only been married a year at the time, and Minerva had just miscarried. I don't know whether Paul wanted it to happen or not, but he had a violent affair with Anna. Alex didn't care for himself, but when Minerva was being hurt, also . . ." Paula sighed. "Anyway, Alex used his influence to send Paul away on a project he had interested himself in in South America, and Anna was forced to return to Athens in his absence." She chewed the side of her cheek with suppressed annoyance. "When Anna developed leukaemia, Alex did everything he could for her. He bought the services of the finest specialists in the world. But it was to no avail. She was incurable, and protesting to the last, she died." Paula stubbed her cigarette out savagely. "I would willingly have strangled her myself," she choked on the words, and lifted her wine with trembling fingers.

"I'm sorry." Dallas felt hopelessly inadequate to comfort the other girl.

Paula managed a slight smile. "I'm sorry, too, but whenever I think about what happened I feel so angry . . ." She bit her lip. "Helen has never married."

"Helen?" Dallas frowned uncomprehendingly.

"Oh, of course, Helen Neroulos. She was Alex's fiancée, the girl he should have married when he married Anna."

"I see." Dallas felt a strange pain in the pit of her stomach.

"Yes. She has been away for a long time. After the engagement was broken, she trained as a doctor and has been working for the last twelve years in Africa. She's quite a woman!"

"She must be," said Dallas, sipping her drink. "Do you think she will ever come back?"

"Oh, yes. During the last month her parents have heard that she plans to come home very shortly. She needs a long holiday, and as the islands have such an idyllic climate, where else would she come but home?"

"Where else?" echoed Dallas softly.

"Mother is enormously pleased, of course," went on Paula. "For years she has wanted to see Alex satisfactorily settled. Now she hopes her wishes may be fulfilled."

"You mean she hopes your brother may now marry this Helen?"

"Of course. After all, Helen is not a child any longer. She's thirty-six, two years younger than Alex, and quite old enough to know her own mind."

Dallas did a swift mental calculation. "Your brother must have been very young when he married Anna."

"Yes, he was. Nineteen, in fact. I was only five years old at the time." She sighed. "This business with your sister and Paris must have reminded him very strongly of that earlier situation. After all, even you must be able to see the similarities."

"Yes, I can," said Dallas, inwardly remembering Alexander's understanding of the circumstances, and how he had attempted to lift all sense of burdening from her and Jane's shoulders. It could not have been easy for him, not when his own marriage had turned out so disastrously as Paula had said. After all, he could quite easily have seen Jane as another Anna, taking the only line to gain what she wanted. Dallas sighed. She didn't want to think of Alexander Stavros like this; she didn't want to feel compassion for him; she wanted to hate him for his arrogance, and for the way he had treated her only a few days ago. But instead she found herself weakening, and wishing most desperately he would return to the island very soon so that she might act a little more tolerantly towards him.

But at this she was again forced to halt herself. It was no good getting close to him. If he once got under her guard, she would be powerless to resist him, and she didn't want to become just another woman to fall stupidly in love with him.

Paula was looking at her strangely. "Dallas," she murmured softly, "you haven't fallen in love with my brother, have you?"

Dallas's eyes were wide as she stared at the older girl. "No," she said violently. "No, *no*, of course I haven't!"

Paula looked rather sceptical as she studied Dallas's suddenly pale cheeks. "Well, be sure you don't," she said quietly. "It would be no good, you know. Alex is not likely to marry anyone except maybe Helen, if he can be manoeuvred into doing so by Mother. And anything else would be fatal for someone like you. You're too nice, too sweet and gentle and loving. You couldn't stand anything less than complete possession, could you?"

"No." Dallas shook her head, and then gave a short laugh. "Oh, Paula," she said, with enforced gaiety, "this is ridiculous, talking like this! Let's talk about you instead. When is this fiancé of yours going to turn up? I'm dying to meet him."

Dallas was aware she was being too effusive, and that it was doubtful that Paula was deceived, even for a moment, but she could not help herself. Somehow she had to shut out all thoughts of Alexander Stavros before they threatened to destroy her.

CHAPTER SEVEN

IT was three weeks before Alexander Stavros returned to Lexandros. During that time both Jane and Dallas managed to achieve a kind of easy acceptance of their situation on the island. Madame Stavros was well pleased that their presence did not interfere in any way with her own arrangements, and both girls were content to remain living a life apart, which had assumed the proportions of a holiday now that they were not required to dress every evening for dinner. Jane was still inclined to grumble sometimes about their hostess, but usually the warmth and colour, the sunshine and the atmosphere of the island worked their own magic, and she spent hours down on the beach below the villa just sunbathing, while Dallas was away teaching the twins.

A week after their arrival on the island, Georges Palamas, Paula's fiancé, arrived. He was a tall blond giant of a man, who good-naturedly treated Dallas and Jane in the same friendly way as he treated Natalia, and often during the late afternoon, when the hours for siesta were over, he would arrive with Paula in the car, to drive down to the cove of Aphrodite. This was a rock-enclosed basin of water, ideal for skin-diving or water-skiing, and although Jane couldn't join in their activities, she didn't seem to mind watching when Georges offered to teach Dallas to water-ski.

The days passed by placidly. Dallas had, with some difficulty, thrust all thoughts of Alexander Stavros to the back of her mind, and in his absence she could almost laugh at the absurdity of her preoccupation with him. After all, it was obvious that he had only been amusing himself with her because she had dared to treat him differently than most other women did, and maybe her attitude had got under his skin. At any rate, she would make sure that nothing like that ever happened again.

Andrea visited them frequently and when he was around Jane brightened considerably. Once, when they were having an evening drink before going to bed, Jane said:

"Andrea has no money, you know," quite thoughtfully.

Dallas stared at her. "What do you mean?"

"Well, I mean, he's not heir to any actual fortune, or anything like that. He will go to England in September to start his university training. When he gets his degree, he hopes to become a civil engineer. He would like to work in South America."

"Oh, I see," Dallas nodded, wondering what else Andrea had told Jane. "You like him very much, don't you?"

Jane smiled. "Yes, I do. He's not like Paris, at least only in looks. He's a much gentler person altogether, and he makes me feel like a real person, not just a stupid teenage girl who's been silly enough to get herself into trouble. I wish he had come to England, not Paris."

"And if he did, how would you have met him?" asked Dallas softly.

"I don't know," Jane sighed. "I sometimes wonder whether it was ordained that I should well . . . well . . . become pregnant, so that we could both come here. I mean, after the baby is born, I'll be a free woman again, won't I?"

Dallas shrugged, lighting a cigarette. "And the baby?"

"Oh, I don't know. Maybe I'll let Alexander Stavros have it after all." Jane looked dejected. "What would you do?"

Dallas shook her head. "That's a question I can't answer. But if I were you I would wait until the baby is born before you start making any rash decisions."

Jane looked pensive, and did not mention the baby again that evening.

One afternoon late in May, when Jane was down on the beach with Andrea, Paula, and Georges, Dallas was surprised when she received an invitation for afternoon tea at the main villa. She had been marking some lesson books of the twins on the patio, relaxing lazily with a cigarette and a glass of iced lime juice which Yanni had brought for her. Reluctantly she went into the chalet, changed into a short pink Crimplene shift and added a coral lipstick to her lips. Already she was tanned a gold brown, and with her colouring it was very attractive. Her hair was coiled into a roll on top of her head, and without taking simply ages there was little she could do to that. So she contented herself by combing the sides into place, becoming annoyed when several tendrils refused to be disciplined, and curled about her ears.

At last she had to leave them, and walked quickly through the trees to the villa with a feeling of suppressed nervousness. She couldn't imagine why she was being summarily summoned like this, and she could only assume she was going to receive a form of reproval from Madame Stavros.

The white-coated manservant showed her into a small sewing-room which opened off the wide hallway. This was one of the smaller rooms in the villa, but even so its proportions were sufficient to dwarf the normal dimensions of any living-room Dallas was used to. The floor was bright with Bokhara rugs of various hues, while the furniture was highly polished mahogany set about with vases of the flowers that grew in abundance in the gardens. Madame Stavros was seated on a Regency striped couch, a small table with a tray of tea in front of her. She smiled welcomingly at Dallas's entrance, and said:

"Ah, my dear, you have come. Tell me, do you take milk and sugar?"

Dallas advanced awkwardly into the room, and seated herself on a low chair near by which Madame Stavros indicated with a flick of her hand.

"Milk only," she said quickly, and accepted the wafer-thin china cup and saucer. Madame Stavros offered her a dish of sweetmeats, known as *loukoumi* or *glyko*, which Dallas had learned were a common accompaniment to refreshments in Greek houses. But she refused anything to eat, still wondering nervously what all this was about.

Madame Stavros helped herself to a Turkish delight from the nearby dish, and then looked thoughtfully at Dallas.

"How are you settling down here?" she asked casually.

Dallas shrugged her shoulders. "Very well, thank you, Madame."

"Good, good." Madame Stavros nodded her head approvingly. "You seem to have captured the hearts of Eloise and Estelle. My son tells me that they look forward to your visits with much pleasure."

"Thank you." Dallas sipped her tea. Was this why she had been brought here? For small talk?

"Yes. This is good, to have an occupation which one enjoys. Few women find their vocation in life. The girl who was to have married my eldest son became a doctor. She is a glowing example of the way one can over-come unhappiness with the application of the mind to other things."

"Oh yes." Dallas refrained from mentioning that Paula had told her about Helen Neroulos.

"Yes." Madame Stavros poured herself more tea. "You will be wondering why I mention this young woman's name, no doubt. It was not without purpose. Helen . . . Helen Neroulos, that is . . . will be returning to the island with my son when he comes home, tomorrow."

Tomorrow! Dallas felt her nerves tauten.

"Yes." Dallas managed the word. Even yet she could not understand the purpose of this conversation.

"Yes. If you are concerned as to why I should be telling you all this, I will get to the point." Madame Stavros bit her lower lip thoughtfully. "Miss Collins, Dallas! You are not a child, a creature of fancies, one might say. You appear to be a perfectly well-balanced young woman." She halted, and sighed. "This is rather difficult for me, my dear, but the fact of the matter is this: it has been apparent from the beginning of your relationship with my eldest son that he has taken upon himself the responsibility not only for your sister but also for you yourself."

Dallas felt her cheeks burning now. She

217

wanted to turn and run but she was forced to remain.

"Yes, Madame," she murmured, stiffening her shoulders.

"Well, this being so, and knowing his innate generosity, I cannot help but fear that you might read more into his concern for yourself than is actually implied by his actions." She rushed on, as she saw Dallas's expression, "My dear, it's you I am thinking about, please believe me. Alexander once made the fatal mistake of marrying the wrong woman; I do not intend that he should be denied this second chance of happiness with the only woman he has ever loved."

"Helen Neroulos," Dallas supplied automatically.

"Of course, Helen." Madame Stavros smiled to herself. "She is perfect for him in every way; her family and ours have been friends and neighbours for generations. She has known Alexander since he was a child, they practically grew up together, and it was always taken for granted that they would eventually marry." Madame Stavros's face darkened. "Then Anna Syros came along and ruined everything!" Her voice was harsh. "I had no love for my son's dead wife. I cannot pretend to have any. She was not the kind of woman to ever marry. Maybe if Alexander had loved her things would have been different, but as it was . . ." Her voice trailed away, and as though remembering to whom she was speaking, she changed the subject. "So Alexander and Helen will be back here tomorrow, and I thought I should try and explain a little of what I hope to happen."

"Oh, you've made everything perfectly clear," said Dallas stiffly, feeling slightly sick. How dared this woman sit here and calmly tell her, in so many words, that her son was not interested in her, Dallas? Even though Dallas knew it for the truth, it had not been necessary to *underline* it. Dallas wanted to cry very badly. Never in her life had she felt so small. How dared Madame Stavros summon her here and warn her off Alexander? As though it was *necessary*! What did she expect Dallas to do? Play the *femme fatale* and distract his attention from his oh-so-perfect fiancée, or almost-fiancée!

Madame Stavros rose to her feet, and Dallas got up too, even though her legs felt as weak as water. But she tightened the hold she was keeping on her emotions, and said: "Is that all, Madame?"

Madame Stavros looked at her intently. "You think all this was unnecessary, don't you?" she said surprisingly.

Dallas twisted her hands together. "Frankly, yes!"

"Then ask yourself why you are feeling so upset now," said Madame Stavros coldly, turning away.

Dallas waited to hear no more. She turned and fled out of the villa, as though the devil himself was at her heels.

★   ★   ★

The tears were streaming down Dallas's cheeks as she ran unheedingly through the trees towards the chalet. There had been so much pent-up emotion during the last few months, and suddenly it had all broken free of the control she had maintained so rigidly. She didn't hear her name being called, or hear footsteps behind her, until strong hands halted that wild abandonment of feeling, and someone hauled her roughly round, and she felt the hard strength of a man's body close against her own. She was sobbing uncontrollably, and for a moment she clung to her captor, not caring who he was, but experienc

220

ing an overwhelming sense of security in his arms. Then she pushed him away and looked up into the dark face of Alexander Stavros.

"Alex," she whispered uncomprehendingly, "but you . . . you're in Athens!"

"*Was* in Athens," he corrected her softly. "And it seems it is high time I came home. What in *hell* has been going on here?"

Dallas took a deep breath, as full realisation of what had just occurred came back to her. She noticed, inconsequently, that he had shaved off his beard, and then she shook her head wildly, and rubbed a childish hand across the tears on her cheeks.

"Tell me," he insisted, still gripping her upper arms with hard fingers.

Dallas shook her head again. "I'm sorry. I was behaving quite ridiculously." She straightened. "Ha . . . have you just arrived?"

"Dallas!" he muttered savagely. "Forget about me. What has been going on? I mean to know, one way or another."

Dallas bent her head, suddenly remembering Helen Neroulos. "You—your mother says you're bringing a visitor with you," she began shakily. "Wh . . . where is she? I hope she doesn't imagine this happens every day." She gave a short humourless laugh.

"Dallas!" Alexander's eyes were dangerously intent upon her. "Please, Dallas, tell me what happened."

"Nothing happened, nothing at all," said Dallas quickly. "Let me go, please. I must go and wash my face before the others come back."

Alexander released her reluctantly, his eyes dark and angry. And then they both became aware that they had a spectator. A woman had walked slowly through the trees towards them, and had halted several yards away, watching them with interested eyes.

Dallas rubbed her cheeks defiantly, and glanced across at the stranger. This must be Helen Neroulos, she thought, feeling a sharp pain in her stomach.

Helen Neroulos was tall, taller even than Dallas, with a slender willowy figure. Her black hair was short, and clung to her head like a cap of ebony, while her dark skin had been tanned deeply by the hot African sun. She was quite beautiful, in a purely classic way, high arched cheekbones moulding a face that would change little with age. She was dressed in slacks and a silk, sleeveless blouse, both in dark green, which suited her dark colouring. A vivid string of fuchsia beads contrasted with her otherwise sombre attire, giving her a startlingly oriental appearance. Dallas hunched her shoulders a little. She ought to have known that the girl Alexander Stavros was expected to marry could be nothing less than extraordinary.

Alexander studied her deliberately for a few moments longer, and then said: "All right, Dallas, we'll talk about this later. Right now I want you to meet a friend of mine, Helen Neroulos. Helen, this is Dallas Collins, Jane's sister."

Helen Neroulos did not shake hands. Instead, she nodded rather languidly, and said: "Darling, I think it would be more kind to introduce me to Miss Collins later. She seems a little . . . how shall I put it . . . disturbed."

Dallas felt she could not stand any more patronising. She was sick of it all; sick of the pretence, and the deliberate manoeuvring, and tired of feeling inferior.

Without a backward glance, she turned and walked quickly away and reaching the sanctuary of her chalet, she entered swiftly, closing the door and turning the key for the first time. Then she heaved a deep breath. This was terrible, and much worse than anything she had ever experienced before. She had made a complete fool of herself, and she felt furiously angry with Alexander Stavros for coming back like that, so unexpectedly, and finding her in such a state. She wanted to pack her cases and leave immediately, and never see any of them ever again, but of course that was impossible. Oh God, she thought wearily. Had she managed to convince Jane that things were not so black for her, only to find her own life impossible? She thought longingly of the steady, uncomplicated existence she had shared with Charles in London. He had never seemed so remote or so understanding. She forgot for a moment his attitude towards Jane, and remembered only the good things; the quiet evenings in the flat, Saturdays at Maidenhead; they all seemed like life on another planet from this distance.

Sighing, she walked through to the bathroom. Maybe a shower would help shed her depression. The lukewarm water cooled her hot skin, and she got Charles's character slowly back into perspective. All her emotional upheaval could not alter the fact that Alexander Stavros was a man, in every sense of the word, and the attraction she felt for him was fast becoming more than a physical thing. Oh, yes, she had to admit it now that she had seen him again; she *was* attracted to him. What had begun as resentment of his arrogance had turned to be a soul-destroying desire to make him wholly aware of her as a woman, as he had been that night at the Temple of Lexa.

She stepped out of the shower angrily. She was breathing quickly, as though she had been running, and there was a feeling of panic invading her being. This was terrible, she thought desperately. Surely the fact that he had kissed her that night before he left proved what kind of man he was! Could she still find herself attracted to him, knowing that that old-fashioned word "intentions" only pointed to dangerous situations? She wrapped the towel round her, and went into her bedroom to find some clean clothes. She, who had found it so easy to criticise Jane, was acting quite ridiculously, even if only in her own thoughts. It just would not do. If he once discovered her weakness she would be lost completely.

Her thoughts turned to Helen Neroulos. She was certainly more the kind of woman he preferred—elegant, soignée, and intelligent, too. That was indeed a rare and stimulating combination. If they did marry and raise a family the children could not fail to inherit both good looks and brains. The wonder of it was that they had waited so long after Anna's death.

Depression settled on Dallas like a cloud. By the time Jane returned, Paula, Andrea, and Georges having returned to the villa, she was seated outside on the patio, reading a magazine, but she felt utterly dejected.

Jane studied her thoughtfully. "You look glum! What's up?"

Dallas shrugged her shoulders. "Nothing. Oh, by the way, Mr. Stavros has returned."

"Alexander?"

"Yes, that's right. I . . . er . . . I had tea with Madame Stavros this afternoon. She sent for me. She told me that he was returning tomorrow and that he was bringing Helen Neroulos with him. She was the woman to whom he was engaged before he married Anna Syros."

"Oh yes," said Jane airily. "I know all about her. Andrea has told me. She's a doctor, isn't she? Andrea said she was coming home from Africa, but he didn't say when." She grimaced. "Is that all Madame said? I

226

wonder why she considered it necessary to inform us? I mean, we don't have much to do with them now, do we?"

Dallas avoided Jane's eyes. "I expect she thought we ought to keep up to date with the visitors to the villa. After all, we do live in the grounds."

"Y . . . e . . . s," Jane shrugged. "Is that what's depressing you?"

"What?"

"The fact that Stavros is coming back tomorrow?"

"Oh no." Dallas spoke quickly. "Anyway, I told you, he's back today, unexpectedly."

"You've *seen* him?"

"Actually, yes."

"Ah!" Jane sounded interested.

"Don't read anything into that," snapped Dallas, aware that she was behaving childishly. "In any case, you're late. You ought to be more careful, really, Jane. You'll be overdoing things again."

"Don't go on," returned Jane irritatedly. "I've told you, I don't particularly care what happens!"

"You don't mean that!"

"Don't I?" Jane flounced into the chalet

and Dallas sighed. Was life ever going to be normal for either of them again?

*　　*　　*

Dallas and Jane ate dinner as usual in the chalet. Their table was drop-leaf, and set beneath the wide windows, from where they could see the curve of the shoreline, and the surging waves on the beach. They had grown used to Greek food, which was superbly cooked in the villa kitchens and brought to them on grill-burners by Yanni. Only Jane had had a slight stomach upset, and this was due, Dallas thought, to her pregnancy. All in all, she had suffered little with the usual sickness associated with pregnancy in its early stages.

This evening, they were both silent as they ate the meal. Jane was annoyed with Dallas for taking too concerned an interest in her condition, and Dallas was furious with herself for becoming engrossed in emotional things.

They were drinking their second cup of coffee when Dallas saw a tall figure walking swiftly through the trees towards their chalet. Even in the gloom it was unmistakable for her; it was Alexander Stavros.

Immediately she became conscious that she had not pinned up her hair but that instead it was loose about her shoulders. After her shower she had combed it out and as she had expected to see no one except perhaps Andrea that evening she had not bothered to fasten it in its knot. Also the dress she was wearing, an old printed cotton of Jane's, was much too short, and her legs were bare. Jane looked at her strangely. "It's Stavros," she said clearly. "I wonder what he wants."

Dallas shook her head. "I wonder."

Jane rose to greet him as he reached the entrance to the chalet.

"Come in," she said, smiling. "Did you have a good trip?"

He entered, and Dallas studied her coffee cup intently, refusing to look at him, knowing how he would look in a dark dinner jacket and trousers cut narrowly to fit his legs.

He smiled at Jane, his eyes flickering to Dallas compulsively. "Yes," he said, "I had a good trip, if a tiring one. And you? How are you?"

"As well as can be expected," she answered tartly. "Isn't that what I'm supposed to say?"

He shrugged his broad shoulders, his lean

face mirroring his absorption with his thoughts. Then he turned to Dallas.

"I want to talk to you," he said bleakly. "Alone."

The record-player was going at the villa tonight, and the sounds of music came plainly over the space between the two dwellings. Dallas could hear the melancholy strains of one of those flowing Ionian *cantades*, a lover's serenade that still had the power to disturb the senses to an awareness of the warmth of the night air, and the multitudinous scents of the flowers. She looked at Alexander without really wanting to, and found his eyes dark and inscrutable upon her.

"I'. . . I don't think we have anything to say to one another," she stammered awkwardly, while Jane stood by, amazed, and marvelling that her calm-and-collected sister should fall apart just because of one man's eyes. This was a side of Dallas she had not known existed, and she felt an overwhelming sense of responsibility suddenly.

"Dallas is tired, Mr. Stavros," she said, moving forward.

Stavros barely glanced at her. "So am I," he muttered coldly. "I have had exactly seven hours' sleep in seventy-two hours."

Dallas stood up hastily. "Surely anything you have to say can be said in front of Jane."

"No. Come, the car is outside. I will take you driving."

"But I'm not ready," exclaimed Dallas. "My hair . . ."

"You look perfectly all right to me," he replied, taking her arm with hard fingers. "Come, I am neglecting my guests."

"And that will never do," murmured Dallas softly, and knew that he had heard by the indrawn breath, and the cruel tightening of his hand on her arm. The suppressed violence about him tonight should have frightened her, but it didn't, it excited her.

Dallas looked at Jane. "Will you be all right?" she asked.

Jane shook her head. "I guess so. Will you?"

Dallas turned back to Alexander Stavros. "All right, I'll come with you. So long as we don't take too long."

"That is understood," he remarked coldly. "I also want to sleep tonight."

Tonight he was driving a dark limousine, a luxurious continental car, that was as soft and comfortable as an armchair to ride in. Dallas slid into her seat, glancing about her. The car was parked near the front entrance to the villa, but apart from the music there was no sign of activity there. Alexander got in beside her, glanced her way once, and then started the powerful engine.

He did not speak as he drove away from the villa, taking a road which Dallas had not been on before. It was little more than a track, and wound away up into the hills in the centre of the island. Here the pines grew thickly, and encroached on to the narrow road. It proved to Dallas that the island was much bigger than she had at first imagined, and this area was possibly used by shooting parties, requiring a day's hunting. There were plenty of birds around, and she supposed they held seasons the same as everyone else.

Her supposition seemed to be proved correct when after a while Alexander brought the car through a gap in the trees, and she saw a pine-logged building, which seemed to be a shooting lodge. Her nerves, distraught as she was, were not helped by this discovery, and she wondered why he had brought her here.

Alexander stopped the car, turned off the engine, and slid out, unbuttoning his collar, and taking off the dress tie he had been wearing.

232

"Come on," he said. "We'll have a drink."

Dallas swallowed hard, hesitated a moment longer, and then climbed out. It was cool up here, and she wished she had brought a cardigan with her. Alexander Stavros was unlocking the door of the cabin, and he pushed it open and went inside. A few moments later a light appeared, and she saw through the window that he had lit two oil lamps. He had also put a match to some logs which had been laid ready in the enormous fireplace, and she could see flames leaping up the chimney. It was a warming and welcoming sight, and Dallas went timidly across the slatted verandah into the beamed-ceilinged room.

Stavros glanced round. "Shut the door," he said. "You'll soon begin to feel warm again."

He seemed to be able to read her thoughts, she thought weakly, and closed the door carefully, without making a sound. Then she moved a little nearer the flames. Already she was beginning to feel warmer, and in consequence more relaxed.

He walked across to a cocktail cabinet, which stood in one corner. Made of small wooden barrels, it blended perfectly with its surroundings, despite the otherwise sporting aspects of the room. Several guns were mounted on the walls, while a selection of fishing rods stood in one corner. The furniture was all leather, and looked well-worn and comfortable. It was a man's room, and she guessed that few women had ever been here.

He poured her a drink, a tall glass filled with a pale green liquid, and she looked distrustingly at it when he handed it to her. "Don't be alarmed," he remarked dryly. "It's mainly lime, but it's combined with vodka. I think you'll find it quite enjoyable." He poured himself a tall glass of lemon juice and Dallas stared at it in astonishment.

He half smiled, albeit a trifle sardonically. "If I drink anything alcoholic I should probably pass out," he remarked lazily. "Feeling as tired as I do I daren't risk it."

"Oh, I see." Dallas sipped her vodka cautiously. "Surely whatever you have to say to me could have waited until tomorrow."

"It could, but I didn't want to wait so long," he replied coolly. He bent over and lifted a thick, long cigar out of a box on the low pine table near the fire. He lit it thoughtfully, and then indicated that she sat down. Dallas shook her head. "I'd rather stand."

Shrugging, he flung himself into a low armchair, the cigar held between his teeth. Dallas thought he had never looked more attractive than he did just then. He was not handsome, his features were too rugged and hard to be called anything so mild as handsome. Instead, he possessed a kind of lean violence, that made Dallas certain that his life had not been the usual cushioned existence of a sybarite. He was used to luxury, it was true, but the character in his features had not been put there by this kind of life. He was hard, not only in character but also as a man, and remembering Charles's soft hands, the hands of an accountant, she felt repelled. If Alexander Stavros had done nothing else he had made her see that there was more to life than merely living.

He leaned his dark head back against the dark leather upholstery, and studied her lazily, his eyes half closed with weariness.

"Come here," he murmured suddenly.

Dallas stiffened, and shook her head. "Please get to the point, Mr. Stavros. If you will say what you've got to say we can go."

He ignored her. "Call me Alex. You did this afternoon."

Dallas turned away, and pretended to be

reading the titles of the books lying on a nearby bookcase. For a while there was silence in the cabin, and Dallas grew tired of studying the books. She turned round, slowly, and then stared at Alexander Stavros with annoyance, blended with amusement at herself. He was asleep, still lying there lazily in front of the now-roaring fire, the cigar burning away between his fingers.

Standing down her own drink, she approached the chair, and removed the cigar from his fingers, stubbing it out in an onyx ashtray near by. Then she looked back at Alexander Stavros. In sleep his features were relaxed and younger, and she looked at him for a long minute. Then she sighed, and taking the chair opposite him she sat down to wait.

It was very cosy in the cabin. The fire lit as well as warmed the room, and getting up, she drew the chintz curtains across the windows, enclosing her in a small world with Alexander Stavros. As she passed his chair again, she looked down at him. It gave her a feeling of contentment somehow, being here with him, like this. She was completely shaken therefore when his fingers suddenly curved round her wrist, pulling her down on top of him.

"Mr. Stavros!" she gasped, trying to free herself.

His eyes were sleepily caressing now. "Oh, Dallas," he murmured passionately, "you're such an adorable creature." His mouth slid softly across the skin of the side of her neck.

Dallas shook her head, breathing quickly. "Please," she said. "It's late."

"I know it. And I'm tired. Let's stay here."

Dallas shook her head more slowly, aching for him to hold her closer against him, as his mouth found hers, gently at first, but then with increasing ardour. Dallas felt her control slipping. The warmth of the room, their isolation up here, away from the rest of the world, all combined to seduce her state of mind so that it was understandable when she wound her bare arms around his neck, and rejoiced when his voice became husky with emotion, as he murmured in her ear in his own language.

Then, as suddenly, she was free, standing on the hearth in front of the fire, and he was over at the cocktail cabinet pouring himself a drink, whisky this time.

She stood there shivering, and he turned and looked back at her, leaning against the cabinet as he swallowed his drink slowly.

Dallas looked into the fire. She felt terrible. She had never thought of herself as an abandoned woman, but with Alexander Stavros, she was, completely.

He straightened and came across to her. "Well?" he murmured. "What are you thinking?"

She looked up. "Do you want the truth?"

"Of course."

"Then I was thinking what an idiot I am. And also I'm sorry you found it necessary to . . . well, show me how foolishly I was behaving!" Her voice was stiff, and he groaned, turning away himself.

"Oh God, Dallas," he muttered. "What a low opinion you have of yourself! Surely you must know how you disturb me! Right now I want to make love to you! And not the kind of half-hearted petting we have been indulging in!"

Dallas twisted her hands together, trembling a little now.

He looked back at her. "But contrary to your imaginings, I do not have an affair with every willing girl that comes along."

He walked to the door. "So come, we go!"

Dallas walked sharply to the door. When they were back in the car, and the cabin was in darkness except for the muted glow of the dying log fire, she said:

"You never told me why you wanted to speak to me."

"No, I never did." He nodded. "All right. Why are you eating in your chalet? Why don't you ever come up to the house? And why were you crying this afternoon?"

Dallas shrugged. "Your . . . your mother prefers it this way, and so do we, actually. It's no good. No matter how friendly people are, we are only here for a transitory time, and with a purpose. We're not *guests* in the accepted sense of the word."

"And the other?"

"This afternoon?"

"Yes. This afternoon!"

Dallas bit her lip. "Oh, it was nothing, really. Maybe I'm too sensitive, but I seem to be putting up with a lot of patronising of late, and I don't like it."

"Is that all?"

"What else is there?"

"You tell me."

"That's all."

He frowned. "I don't believe you."

"I can't make you. Look, I'm cold. Can we go?"

Alexander looked at her angrily, and for a moment she thought he was going to force her to tell him by brute methods. But then he raised his shoulders in a lazy manner, and started the powerful car.

The journey back was accomplished in silence, and Dallas was glad. She didn't understand him; it was impossible for her to do so. He wanted her, that much she knew, but that was nothing really. He didn't care for her in any other way. Not like she cared for him.

She felt a wave of nausea overwhelm her. It was no good fighting against the truth any longer. She wasn't just attracted to Alexander Stavros; she was in love with him, hopelessly, helplessly, and irrevocably.

CHAPTER EIGHT

TWO days later Jane told her she was going sailing with Andrea.

Dallas looked at her sister anxiously. "Sailing? In your condition!"

"Oh, don't start that again, Dallas. After all, what's wrong with sailing anyway, in any condition?"

"Andrea's boat, it's only a sailing vessel!"

"I know. But it's a glorious day, and perfect for sailing. He says we won't go far. Just out in the channel, between here and Viryous." Viryous was the neighbouring island where Helen Neroulos's parents lived.

Since her arrival with Alexander Stavros, Helen had spent little time on her own island, preferring instead to stay at the villa, and the two girls had seen her with Alexander and Nikos, swimming and driving away to go skin-diving. Dallas had not seen Alexander since the night at the cabin, and she could only assume that he was avoiding her. Not that she minded; seeing him was torture anyway.

But now she was faced with the problem of

Jane again. "Honestly, Jane, I wish you wouldn't go," she said evenly. "I mean, what if the boat capsized?"

"Capsized? In this weather?" It was a glorious day, with only a gentle breeze tugging at the leaves of the olive trees.

"Oh, all right." Dallas shook her head. "I can't stop you if you're determined."

"That's for sure," said Jane defiantly, and went inside the chalet to collect her things.

Dallas left soon afterwards to go to Paul Stavros's home for her lessons with Eloise and Estelle, but despite their chatter she could not rid herself of a faint feeling of unease where Jane was concerned.

When she got back to the chalet, Jane had not returned, but there was a note from her propped up on the table. It said:

"We're taking lunch with us. Don't expect us back before five."

Dallas sighed, screwed the note up and dropped it into the waste bin. Then she showered and changed into slim-fitting slacks and a long-sleeved chiffon blouse. It was very hot, a kind of humid heat that was unlike anything she had experienced since coming to the island.

She looked up at the sky, and saw that

instead of its usual blue it was a kind of yellowish purple, which must surely herald a storm. A *storm*! Her heart turned over. And Andrea and Jane were out there, sailing!

She looked at her watch. It was almost two o'clock. Surely they would turn for home when the weather changed. But what if they didn't? What if there was no wind? What if they were stranded somewhere out in the bay?

Yanni arrived with her lunch, but she had no stomach for food.

"Yanni," she said, "where is Mr. Stavros? Mr. Alexander Stavros?"

Yanni frowned. "He having lunch at the villa," he said, nodding comfortably. "You want see him?"

Dallas thought of saying "yes", but then changed her mind. If she summoned Alexander Stavros here, it would seem like the cat calling the king. No, she would have to go up to the villa herself, and ask to speak to him.

"Thank you, Yanni," she said. "I'll see about it myself."

When she reached the villa she entered the entrance hall nervously, and was further dismayed when Madame Stavros came out of the lounge and came to meet her. "Yes?" she said coldly. "Can I help you?"

"No, thank you. I want to speak to Mr. Stavros."

Madame Stavros compressed her lips. "He is busy at the moment. Surely I can deal with it, whatever it is."

"I'm afraid not." Dallas was firm.

Their voices must have penetrated the dining-room, for a moment later Alexander emerged. Dressed in a polo-necked blue shirt, and close-fitting cream pants, he looked painfully disturbing. His eyes narrowed when he saw Dallas.

"What's wrong?" he asked, frowning. "Dallas, what's wrong?"

Dallas was so relieved to see him that her voice was warmer than she intended. "Andrea has taken Jane sailing," she said bluntly. "And . . . and I think there's a storm blowing up."

Alexander stared at her intently. "Yes, there is. Crazy fool! God, Mother, does Andrea have no sense?"

Madame Stavros looked bored by the whole business. "Actually, I suggested it," she replied coldly. "Andrea wanted to go sailing. He asked whether it would be suitable to take Jane. I said yes."

"You did what!" Alexander stared at her angrily. "If anything happens to her, I'll personally hold you responsible!"

For the first time Dallas saw Madame Stavros disconcerted. Her pale cheeks gathered a little hot colour, and she looked irritatedly at Dallas as though all this were her fault.

"Don't talk like that, Alex," she said, taking his arm. "Nothing is going to happen!"

Alexander shook off her hands, and then Nikos appeared. Dallas had not seen much of him since his return, and she wondered whether Madame Stavros had warned him off, too. Nikos smiled warmly at Dallas, and murmured:

"What's this? A family conference?"

Alexander ignored him. He was frowning as he tried to sort out the best thing to do. Then he looked at Dallas and said:

"I'll take out the schooner. Nik, you can crew for me. We'll have to manage alone, unless Helen wants to come, too." His eyes were gentle on Dallas. "Do you want to come?"

"May I?"

Madame Stavros was stiff and unyielding, her face a disapproving mask.

"I think this is a storm over nothing," she exclaimed impatiently. "Alex darling, you haven't finished your meal!"

Alexander gave her a long considering look, and she bent her head. Then he turned and walked back into the dining-room, presumably to see Helen. Madame Stavros followed him rather more slowly, and Nikos took Dallas's arm and led her outside.

"What's going on?" he asked softly. "Al sure looks mad!"

Dallas explained as briefly as she could. Then, shifting her thoughts with difficulty, she said: "How are you? Long time, no see."

Nikos grinned. "And *you* know why," he murmured, darkly, his eyes appraising her thoroughly.

"*I do?*"

"Sure." Nikos lit a cigarette. "If I step on big brother's toes, I get my fingers rapped, so I don't!"

Dallas frowned in amazement. "You mean—Alex?"

"Now don't tell me you didn't know." Nikos looked disbelieving. "Anyway, if you'd just spent two weeks in his company, and suffered the knife-edge of his tongue on more than one occasion, simply because

246

some girl was riding him, you'd see my point."

Dallas shook his head. "I'm not that girl," she said definitely.

"No?" He shrugged. "Well, why did I get the "hands off" treatment?"

Dallas was incredulous. "I don't know."

Nikos gave her a sardonic look. "Oh, well, as I said, I'm all for the peaceful life." He smiled. "But believe me, it was not my idea."

"I thought it was your mother's," exclaimed Dallas impulsively.

"Did you? Well, believe me, honey, Alex was letting some woman bug him while we were away, and the night before we left he came home in one hell of a temper. And he had been with you, hadn't he? My mother knew that!"

Dallas felt hot all over. This explained a lot of things; particularly Madame Stavros's preoccupation with telling her who was coming home with Alexander.

Then behind them were footsteps and Alexander appeared accompanied by Helen Neroulos. She was wearing a tangerine-coloured slack suit, and looked as elegant and sophisticated as ever. She smiled condescendingly at Dallas, and said: "So we meet again,

Miss Collins. It seems your life is a series of crises!"

Nikos grinned at Dallas at this, and took the sting out of Helen's words. Dallas managed to smile back at him, and then they went down the steps and round to the side of the house where a low-slung convertible was parked.

The schooner *Athena* was long and luxurious, two-masted, and compact enough for four persons. There were two cabins and a galley, as well as a small bathroom. Alexander did not use the sails, but instead started the vessel's motor and turned it out into the bay.

Already the sea was green and choppy, and Dallas felt her empty stomach begin to churn a little. She had never tested her reactions to rough water, her trips across the Channel being confined to calm weather. It was only a small vessel, compared to these pleasure cruisers, and she felt very tense and frightened.

All the fishing boats and the sloops and caiques were making for the harbour. They were the only ones heading out. Dallas leaned on the rail, concentrating on the horizon. She had heard that this relieved seasickness. Nikos came to lean beside her, smiling at her tense features.

248

"Relax," he said smilingly. "They'll be okay. It's you I'm worried about."

Dallas managed a faint smile, wondering frantically what she would do if she was sick. It would be terrible to make a fool of herself in front of Helen Neroulos, who was standing beside Alexander in the wheel-house quite casually, looking as though she was used to any kind of weather conditions.

But their journey seemed to be in vain. There was no sign of Jane and Andrea and the yacht, and Alexander looked a trifle disturbed now. Nikos had left Dallas to go and make some coffee, and Alexander came to take his place, leaving Helen in charge of the wheel. He studied her pale cheeks and said:

"You're feeling rotten, aren't you?"

Dallas nodded, tightening her fingers on the rail.

"Why on earth did you come, then?" he asked, biting his lip.

Dallas grimaced. "Oh, I didn't know I was going to feel like this," she said shakily. "I've never sailed in rough seas before."

He grinned at this, and leaned his back against the rail beside her, resting his elbows on the bar. "You're perfectly safe, you know," he said gently. "We won't capsize, or anything like that."

"That's a great relief," murmured Dallas dryly, and he shrugged and walked away.

Dallas was not actually sick, but she was wonderfully relieved when at last they returned to the harbour. It had started to rain now, and the wind was sending the clouds racing across the sky. She looked worriedly at Alexander, and he said:

"Don't worry yet. The fact that we've not seen them is a good thing."

"Or very bad," remarked Helen thoughtlessly.

But on the quay, Madame Stavros waited in the dark limousine that Alexander had used the night he took Dallas up to the lodge in the hills. She slid out at their appearance, and waved vigorously.

Alexander looked at Dallas. "She has news," he said, "and it's obviously good news or she wouldn't be here."

"Thank goodness!" murmured Dallas fervently.

When they reached Madame Stavros she wasted no time in telling them what had happened. "When the weather changed they went into the harbour at Viryous. Helen's mother has just telephoned to say they are there. Perfectly all right, and staying for dinner. If the weather doesn't change, they'll stay overnight."

"Oh, that's a relief!" Dallas pressed a hand to her stomach.

Madame Stavros looked at her coldly. "You see, Miss Collins, there was no need for such dramatics," she said.

Dallas shook her head, but Alexander's eyes were cold as he looked at his mother. "That hardly alters the fact that it could have been potentially dangerous," he said. "Dallas was right to come and tell me."

Nikos nudged her gently in the small of her back, and Dallas moved quickly away from him.

"Come," said Alexander. "We can go back now. It is no use standing here, getting soaked."

They all got back in the cars, and drove back to the villa, Dallas in the back of Alexander's car with Nikos, while Helen rode in front. Once there, she excused herself, and ran across to the chalet. Again she seemed to have made a fool of herself, and she felt utterly depressed.

★　★　★

A week later Alexander Stavros left for Athens again, leaving Nikos behind, this time. Helen had returned to Viryous, and life resumed its normal tenor. Dallas had not seen him alone before he left, Madame Stavros had seen to that by arranging various dinner-parties and the house was always full of guests.

Dallas had tried to avoid him, anyway. Whenever he came to the chalet, as he frequently did, to ask after Jane's health, she made a point of either being in the bath or the shower, and there had been no more painful episodes. She could only presume that his attraction towards her had petered out, due no doubt to the fact that she had shown how pliable she was in his expert hands. Besides, Helen monopolised his time, and as she treated both girls with amiable condescension there was no question of them becoming involved in the personal affairs at the villa.

It was about three days after Alexander's departure that Jane announced that she was going sailing with Andrea again. Dallas heaved a huge sigh.

"Oh, Jane, not again, please!"

Jane gave an angry exclamation. "Honestly, Dallas, you're beginning to annoy me? What do you imagine is going to happen to me? I can look after myself. Besides, Andrea is perfectly capable of taking me sailing without mishap."

"You know very well that, Alexan . . . Mr. Stavros told Andrea he was never to take you sailing again!"

"Alexander, eh?" Jane folded her arms mockingly. "My, my, what slipped out then?"

"Jane, stop it!" Dallas turned away. "Do you imagine I'm thinking of myself in this?"

"I don't know," said Jane consideringly. "You might be. After all, if *Alexander* has spoken, who knows what you may have promised!"

"Jane!"

"Well, it's true." Jane looked sulky. "You seem to be having a great time here on the quiet. Heavens, he can't wait to see you alone the minute he arrives on the island, even though he's practically dead on his feet, and then he takes you off for a couple of hours to some place in the hills where goodness knows what happened!"

"Jane!" Dallas felt sick. "Stop it!"

"Well, it's true. You can't deny it, can you? What goes on with you two? I'd lay odds that it's no platonic friendship!"

Dallas turned away, and shook her head violently. "You don't know what you're saying."

"Don't I? Maybe not, but I dare bet that after Charles Jennings Alexander Stavros is pretty hot stuff." She smiled maliciously. "Heavens, I can think of at least half a dozen women who would give their right hand to be in your position here."

"Perhaps you can," said Dallas evenly, disguising the hurt she was feeling at Jane's careless words. "Anyway, are you going?"

"Sailing? Of course I am." She stretched lazily. "In a month or so Andrea won't want to be seen dead with me, when I start looking ghastly! But right now, he enjoys my company, and quite frankly I *love* his."

"*Love!*" Dallas looked sceptical. "That word comes too easily to you, Jane. Not everything comes under that heading, you know."

"If you've found that out, it wasn't from Charles Jennings," remarked Jane insolently. "Well, I must get ready, *darling*," imitating Helen's lazy drawl. "See you!"

Dallas went to her work as usual, feeling depressed and anxious. It seemed obvious that in Alexander's absence, Madame Stavros depressed and anxious. It seemed obvious in Alexander's absence, Madame Stavros was giving the answers, and naturally she didn't particularly care what happened to either of them.

It was about eleven-thirty when the telephone call came through. Dallas was in the garden with Eloise and Estelle. They were cataloguing the various flowers, and the twins thought it a marvellous pastime. When Minerva came hurrying out of the villa to speak to her, Dallas still did not attach any significance to her worried face.

"Dallas!" Minerva looked at her compassionately. "That was a call from Paul's mother. . . ."

At last realisation that something was wrong dawned. Dallas stared at her in dismay. "Something's happened to Jane!" she cried, feeling suddenly very young, and very scared.

Minerva stared at her in her turn. "You knew!"

"No, I guessed. She went sailing with Andrea this morning. What happened? Did the boat capsize?" She was aware that tears were running down her cheeks now.

Minerva put a comforting arm about her

shoulders. "No, darling, nothing like that. They . . . they crashed, in Andrea's car, on their way to the village."

"Oh no!" Dallas covered her face with her hands.

"Yes, my dear. It must have happened some time ago, but there has been so much confusion Madame Stavros couldn't let us know sooner."

Or wouldn't, thought Dallas, and then stifled the thought.

"And where is Jane now?" she asked. "Is she badly hurt? Is she *dead*?"

"Oh no, Dallas, not dead! She's hurt, both of them were hurt. They've been rushed to hospital in Athens in the plane. Darling, don't worry! I know that's easy to say at a time like this, but really, Madame Stavros says she is sure they will both be all right."

Dallas wiped her tears with the back of her hand. "Oh, God!" she said, shaking her head. "If only there was someone . . . someone I could turn to!" She felt contrite at once as she saw Minerva's expression. "Please understand, Minerva," she said softly. "We have no father; our mother ran away when we were both children; there's no one else!"

"I know." Minerva patted her shoulder

gently. "Come on. Simeon can take you back to the villa. You'll want to see Madame Stavros and find out for yourself what has happened. I'm sorry I had to be the bearer of such bad news."

Dallas managed a smile, and nodding she said goodbye to the twins and climbed into the car. As it sped back towards the Stavros villa she felt utterly weary. If Jane got out of this alive, she would be remarkably lucky considering the narrow escape she had had once before with Paris.

Madame Stavros awaited her in the lounge of the villa. With her were Paula and Natalia, the latter looking less confident than she usually did. She spoke in a low voice to Dallas, and then Madame Stavros said:

"You'll have heard from Minerva what happened."

"Yes, I heard," Dallas nodded, not trusting herself to say more. "Where are they?"

"They are at the Sisters of Mercy Hospital in Athens," replied Madame Stavros heavily. "It's a new building, very modern and up to date, with the best specialists in Greece on hand should they be required. Nikos and Doctor Zantes have gone with them in the plane. We telephoned ahead. An ambulance will be waiting for them at the airport." She glanced at her watch. "Actually, they should be there by now. They left some time ago."

"And didn't you think I should have been first to be informed?" asked Dallas chokily. "I mean, after all, Jane is my sister."

Madame Stavros stiffened. "I do not think you could have done anything useful," she replied coldly. "Neither of them were conscious when they left."

"Oh!" Dallas pressed a hand to her lips. "Were they badly . . . I mean . . . what were their injuries?"

"It was impossible to tell without X-rays," said Paula gently. "Andrea had a cut on his head, which bled rather a lot, but otherwise he seemed all right. Jane didn't appear to have any superficial injuries apart from cuts and bruises, but . . . well . . ." Her voice trailed away. "You'll find out when you go."

"And when can I go?" asked Dallas, looking from one to another of them. "Have . . . have you let Alexander know?" This was no time for pretending.

"Of course." Madame Stavros spoke. "I telephoned his hotel first of all. He is in Athens. He will be at the hospital when they arrive. They told me to tell you that he would be back here later this afternoon."

Dallas breathed a sigh of relief. Just now, Alexander Stavros seemed the only rock she had to cling to, and she badly wanted to see him.

"Did you speak to him?" she asked.

Madame Stavros shook her head. "I spoke to Stephanos," she replied. "Naturally, Alexander was busy. But he would get the message, don't worry."

Dallas turned away. Just now worry was all she could do.

★　　★　　★

It was late in the afternoon when Dallas heard the sound of a jet overhead. It seemed to be circling prior to landing, and she came out of the chalet, looking up expectantly. Jets didn't normally land on Lexandros, in fact Nikos had said the runway wasn't long enough. But this one was coming down, and she put a hand to her throat nervously. If this was Alexander, she prayed he would get down safely.

The sound was deafening in the still heat of the afternoon air, and Dallas went inside again, and lit a cigarette with trembling fingers. Then she looked at her reflection in the mirror above the sideboard. Apart from vaguely dark lines below her eyes, due to the fact that she was not sleeping too well just now, she looked much the same as usual. She sighed, smoothing a hand over her hair which hung loosely to her shoulders. She had not had the patience to reset it after her shower. She had put on a royal blue skirt with a deeply inverted pleat at the front, and a knitted nylon sweater, with short sleeves and a low V-neckline. She wore no make-up, but now lifted her lipstick and applied some to her trembling lips.

Then she walked back to the door, and out on to the patio. Heat shimmered over everything; it was a perfect day. A perfect day for sailing, in fact. She sighed deeply. The car crash had been something she had never even imagined. Her earlier forebodings had been justified, but quite differently from her expectations.

Realising she was smoking too much, she lit yet another cigarette, and paced about the tiled floor area restlessly. Soon she heard the sound of a car's powerful engine, and she stamped out her cigarette and walked through the trees to the road, lower than the villa, along the drive. The white Mercedes turned into the drive, throwing up a fine dusty spray, as the tyres squealed slightly in protest. Dallas stepped back, but the Mercedes swished to a halt only a couple of feet away from her, and almost before it had stopped, the door opened and Alexander slid out. She had a fleeting yet comprehensive appraisal of his dark masculinity, enhanced by a biscuit-coloured lounge suit and cream shirt, then he had gripped her arms and said:

"Hello, honey. Are you all right?"

Dallas gazed at him mutely, then buried her face in his chest, allowing the tears which she had been bottling up to flow unrestrainedly. Alexander let her cry for a few moments, turning his head and indicating that the chauffeur should take the car up to the villa and inform his mother that he had arrived. Then he gently but firmly held her away from him, and said: "Come on, Dallas, things aren't as black as all that. Look, let's go up to the house. I've got to tell my mother what's happened, and then we're leaving. Right?"

Dallas nodded, wiping her eyes with the handkerchief he held out to her, and then walking with him up the drive, his arm casually across her slim shoulders, his head bent to hers.

"We certainly seem to be causing you a lot of trouble," she said tightly, twisting the handkerchief in her fingers.

I'll go along with that," he murmured, half mockingly. "Never mind. I guess I'll survive!"

Madame Stavros, together with her two daughters, waited at the top of the steps, and watched Alexander and Dallas walk up the drive together. Madame Stavros's face was drawn and anxious, and her expression darkened when she saw her son with Dallas.

"Well?" she said. "Have you seen Andrea?"

Alexander removed his arm from Dallas, and walked easily up the steps to his mother's side. "Yes," he said, "I've seen *Jane* and Andrea."

"How are they?" It was Natalia.

"They'll live," he said noncommittally. "Andrea is only concussed, with a broken bone in his elbow. Jane has multiple cuts and bruises, and is also slightly concussed."

Dallas mounted the steps unsteadily. "The . . . the . . . baby. . . ."

Alexander's eyes darkened. "There's not

going to be any baby," he said softly. "I'm sorry."

Dallas stood motionless, and then she shivered violently. She had known, of course, before she asked the question. Jane could not possibly have two accidents without causing harm to the unborn child.

She ran a tongue over her lips. "Does . . . does Jane know?"

Alexander nodded. "She came round in the plane. She knew then."

Dallas nodded, and turned away. She wanted to be sick, but she was empty inside. Alexander shook his head as Paula would have gone to her. Instead, he took her arm and led her across the hall into a small study, where he poured her a glass of brandy, only slightly laced with soda, and instructed her to drink it.

Dallas did as she was bidden. The raw spirit warmed her inside, and dispelled momentarily the utter despair she seemed to be experiencing. She was handed a cigarette, already lit, and she saw him light himself a thick cigar. Then he flung himself into the swivel chair behind the desk which dominated the room, and swung it silently backwards and forwards, watching her intently.

After she had managed to swallow most of it, he stood up.

"I'll tell my mother we are leaving," he said. "Wait here."

Dallas felt like one sleep-walking. She was glad she had Alexander there to think for her; her mind felt completely muzzy.

Later, in the car going down to the airstrip, she roused herself sufficiently to ask: "Was that your plane? The jet?"

Alexander turned round to look at her. He was sitting in front with Simeon, the chauffeur, while Dallas had the back to herself.

"Yes, that was mine," he nodded. "It's the company jet."

"The company? . . . oh, you mean the Stavros shipping company."

"That's right." Alexander swung round again, and Dallas stared out of the window rather blindly.

"Nikos said a jet couldn't land here," she murmured thoughtfully.

Alexander gave a short laugh. "He's almost right. But I have the best pilot in the world at the controls. He could put a plane down on an ice-floe." He glanced at Simeon. "You didn't think he'd make it."

264

Simeon shook his head, and said something in Greek.

The company jet was a twin-engined aeroplane, and inside it was laid out like a luxurious office-cum-bar. There was a desk, a telephone, plenty of armchairs, and a cocktail bar. After take-off, which was nerve-racking for Dallas because she knew that the strip was not long enough, and that it took the utmost skill to get the powerful aircraft into the air, she managed to relax a little. They were on their way, and there was nothing she could do now but wait.

She accepted a drink and a cigarette, and studied Alexander as he lay back in the chair by the desk studying some technical charts and papers. He ignored her the whole of the trip, and she could only assume that they had interrupted his working schedule. She read a couple of magazines disinterestedly, and thought a lot. There was nothing else to do. It was fantastic really to imagine they were thousands of feet up in the clouds in a pressurised cabin, when this looked nothing more than an office.

As they neared Athens Dallas realised that now there was to be no baby, once Jane had recovered there would be nothing to keep them in Greece. Her cheeks paled at the thought, and Alexander, glancing at her then, said:

"What's wrong? Do you feel sick?"

Dallas shook her head. "No, I'm all right, thank you."

He frowned, but shrugging, he returned to his papers. When the plane landed another sleek chauffeur-driven limousine awaited them, this time with the circled monogram of the Stavros Shipping Line clearly marked on the forward doors. Dallas supposed this was executive treatment, the kind of treatment Alexander Stavros was used to. An executive jet, and an executive limousine. She glanced at him as they walked across the tarmac to the waiting car. Stephanos Karantinos had come to meet them, and he and Alexander talked together as they walked to the car. Watching Alexander, she thought that this was a side of him she really knew little about. In the relaxed atmosphere of the island she was wont to forget the position he held, but here, among his subordinates, no one could have mistaken him for anything else. He was well-groomed, assured, and conscious of the power he wielded with such success.

Dallas had her first sightseeing tour of

Athens in the executive car. This time she sat in front, while Stephanos and Alexander sat together in the back. Despite her depression and anxiety she could not fail to appreciate the symmetrical moulding of modern buildings with ancient monuments. Choked with traffic, Dallas thought she had never seen so many buses in her life, it nevertheless maintained its individuality and magnificence, the soaring skyscrapers of hotels and shops and apartment buildings detracting little from the purely classical sense of history, and majesty.

She stared through the windows wide-eyed, the sights and sounds flooding her eyes and ears to the exclusion of all else. It was a pity, she thought, that she would not have a chance to explore Athens more fully. There was so much to see, and she was her father's daughter; archaeology had always excited her.

They skirted the centre of the city, and came upon the newly built hospital of the Sisters of Mercy in a street just off the *Leoforos Amalias*. It had a small car-park, and the chauffeur stopped the car and they all got out.

Alexander spoke to Stephanos in an undertone, and he nodded, and smiled encouragingly at Dallas. Alexander took Dallas's arm, and in no time at all they were walking through the marble-tiled entrance hall and being directed to the private rooms where Andrea and Jane were resting.

A lift transported them to the fourth floor, and the nurse who had accompanied them led them down the corridor to the far end where another nurse, obviously a ward Sister or something, Dallas assumed, took them first to see Jane.

Jane was lying, looking pale and listless in the narrow hospital bed, her hair, which had been long like Dallas's, now cut short to enable the doctors to deal with two head wounds. She seemed to be a mass of bandages, and Dallas had to force herself not to show anxiety.

"Hello, love," she said, sitting down beside her, while Alexander went outside with the nurse. "How do you feel?"

Jane looked at her sister, and then her face crumpled up and she burst into tears. "I've lost my baby," she sobbed, pulling Dallas towards her, and burying her face in her sister's neck.

Dallas let her cry. After all, that was

probably the best thing she could do. Only getting it out of her system in this way would she be able to make any real recovery.

After a long while Jane became silent, and drew back, looking ashamed.

"I'm sorry, Dallas," she said quietly. "I've been an absolute idiot. You have every right to really let go at me!"

Dallas sighed, taking Jane's hands. "Don't be silly. I'm only grateful that you're all right . . . otherwise. You are all right, aren't you?"

"Oh yes, perfectly. My concussion isn't even as severe as Andrea's. Have you seen him?"

"Not yet. I expect we will, later."

"How did you get here? Did Mr. Stavros send for you?"

"No. He came for me, in a *jet*!" Dallas managed a light laugh. "Just imagine, executive treatment, for *us*!"

"He was marvellous when he came to see me this afternoon," said Jane, gripping Dallas's hands very tightly. "He told me I hadn't a thing to worry about. That he would see I didn't suffer because of . . . well, because of this."

Dallas stiffened a little. "You realise we'll

have to return to London now, once you've recovered."

Jane looked less happy now. "Why?"

"Oh, Jane, don't be silly. You know perfectly well *why*."

"Don't trouble Jane with your plans right now," murmured a voice behind her, and Dallas sprang up to face Alexander. She twisted her hands together, and said:

"Sooner or later we'll have to leave. It's no use pretending about it."

"We'll talk about it," he said quietly, and then looked at Jane. "Well, Jane, how do you feel now?"

"Woozy," said Jane, smiling a little. "But I'll recover."

"I'm sure you will." He nodded kindly, and then said: "The Sister says we should not stay too long. Jane has been given a sedative, and will probably sleep for a while. You'll see her tomorrow."

After leaving Jane they went into Andrea's room. He looked much weaker than Jane, and could hardly open his eyes. But he looked shamefully distressed, and said, a little thickly:

"I'm sorry, Dallas. I don't know what you and Jane must think of me. I've made an absolute mess of everything."

Dallas found it was terribly easy to forgive Andrea. He was obviously so upset, and she leant over him smiling, and murmured: "Don't worry. I don't place blame on people. I guess it wasn't ordained that she should have the child. Maybe it's just as well."

Andrea looked a little comforted, and when they were going down in the lift again, Dallas looked at Alexander thoughtfully. "You don't suppose this anxiety of Andrea's will retard his progress, do you?"

Alexander looked half amused. "No, I don't think so. Not now, at any rate. You certainly relieved his mind. Thank you. I'll have a few well-chosen words to say to that young man myself when he's fit to hear them."

"Oh no!" Dallas put a hand on his arm, and then as he bent his head and looked at it, she quickly withdrew it. "I mean . . . wait and see how Jane progresses."

He lifted his shoulders, and then they were outside in the excitingly scented night air. He lifted the white jacket she was carrying, and placed it about her shoulders, and then said:

"Come on, we'll walk. I want to show you *my* Athens."

"But . . . I mean . . . the car . . .?"

271

"Stephanos will see to all that," he remarked lazily.

"And tonight? Are we going back to the island?"

"No."

Dallas stared at him. "No?" she echoed faintly.

He smiled down at her. "Don't be alarmed. I've booked you a room in a very respectable hotel."

"*Your* hotel?"

"No, not my hotel. Don't worry, I shan't be around to disturb your beauty sleep."

Dallas glanced at him helplessly, wondering what the situation would have been if it were Helen Neroulos here with him in Athens. She felt hopelessly out of her depth and with burning cheeks she turned and walked quickly away down the street, looking back to find him following her with long lazy strides.

That evening in Athens Dallas experienced a little taste of what living there was really like. They avoided the huge, noisy restaurants patronised by the tourists, and instead he took her to a *taverna* near the Plaka, where they sat outside under the stars, eating fish that fell apart in their fingers, and drinking the sweet Greek wine in tall beakers. This was yet another side to Alexander Stavros. Wherever they went he was recognised, but not as the owner of the Stavros Shipping Line, but as a man, a man, moreover, that they liked and respected. They listened to the music of the entertainers inside, and then stood watching the men dance the *zeimbekiko*. The Greeks seemed the most effervescent race Dallas had ever known, and the singing and laughter and constant chatter obliterated for a while her own unhappiness. Alexander was more relaxed than she had ever seen him, and afterwards they walked to the foothills of the Acropolis, feeling almost part of the whole scene.

Then it was very late, and Alexander summoned a cab, and they drove to Dallas's hotel. She stared in trepidation at the imposing façade of the Athens Hilton, and then shook her head at Alexander.

"I—I couldn't stay here!" she gasped.

"Come," he said, ignoring her protestations. "Don't be alarmed, I will take you to your suite."

Dallas had no option but to follow him, but her trepidation increased when she saw the opulence of her surroundings. She had never had a suite all to herself before, and she stood in the centre of the lounge looking lost and vulnerable suddenly.

Alexander stood by the door watching her through narrowed eyes, and then he said, with a kind of impatience, "Relax, Dallas. Don't underestimate yourself. You'll find it's not so terrifying."

"You're wrong," she said, hugging herself tightly. "You forget, I'm not Helen Neroulos!"

She didn't know why she had to mention that woman's name, but it was out, and she felt hot and embarrassed.

Alexander gave her a long look. "I know who you are," he murmured, and then turned away and went down the hall away from her. Dallas ran and closed the door leaning back against it, her eyes closed.

CHAPTER NINE

DALLAS did not see Alexander Stavros again for four days. The morning after their visit to the *taverna*, Stephanos arrived at the hotel with a message to the effect that Alexander wanted Dallas to remain in Athens for the next few days, some of her clothes were being sent for, and Stephanos had been given the job of looking after her.

"Oh, but really . . ." began Dallas, looking disturbed. "I mean—you don't need to bother about me. I can easily get myself a cab when I go to the hospital to see Jane. I'm not completely incapable." She felt angry that Alexander should have again asserted his control over her. Did he think she needed a bodyguard? Simply because he was not around! In her emotionally unstable condition she could hardly assimilate things sensibly and normally.

But Stephanos merely grinned tolerantly at her outburst, and said: "Have you breakfasted? Good. Then get your coat and we'll go."

"Go?" Dallas stared at him. "Go where? To the hospital? Is something wrong?" Her cheeks paled.

Stephanos shook his head vigorously. "Nothing's wrong! We're going sightseeing, that's all. That's what you'd like to do, isn't it?"

She stared at him. "Are you serious?"

"Sure. Why not? After all, I've been given instructions to keep you happy! What other way could I oblige?" he grinned.

Dallas had to smile at this, and lifted the weight of her hair off the back of her neck thoughtfully. "All right," she said. "Just give me five minutes. I've got nothing else to change into, I'm afraid."

"You will have, later," he remarked lazily. "Hurry up."

Those days in Athens Dallas found pleasantly uncomplicated. Stephanos was an amusing and interesting companion, but he made no demands on her, and she was able to relax with him and find that acting like all the other tourists could be very enjoyable. She saw all the famous archaeological sights, the museums and parks; they went window-shopping along Stadium Street and visited the harbours. Dallas saw the sleek, white-painted yachts moored at *Pasha Limani,* they drank aromatic Turkish coffee in the restaurant there. Naturally they spent longest at the Acropolis, Dallas trailing round after the guide while Stephanos rested his tired feet on a low wall, smoking, and looking on with good-natured amusement.

In the evenings they went to the *tavernas,* and Dallas joined in the general air of festivity. It was only when she was back in the quiet of her rooms at the hotel that a kind of depressing misery overcame her, and she cried herself to sleep more than once.

At the hospital, Jane made good progress. She was up and about again, and had been told she could leave at the end of the week. Andrea was staying a few days longer, owing to the fact that he had had stitches in his head and they would not let him leave without removing them.

When Dallas went to see Jane it was impossible to pin down the conversation to their future plans. Jane refused to consider what they were going to do, and kept on saying that there was plenty of time. Dallas was less confident; they had never really been accepted by Madame Stavros, and she doubted very much whether Alexander's mother would expect them to return to the island at all.

However, the day before Jane was due to leave the hospital Alexander himself arrived while Dallas was with her sister. Dallas felt her heart throbbing sickeningly when he walked with easy grace into the room, and she marvelled that her body could stand the strain. But not much more, she thought achingly. She had to get *away*!

He spoke to Dallas and then smiled at Jane. "Well?" he said. "I hear you're being discharged tomorrow."

Jane nodded. "Yes, thank goodness."

He looked thoughtfully at Dallas's bent head, and then looked again at Jane. "Stephanos will pick you up at ten-thirty," he said. His eyes returned to Dallas. "He'll pick you up at your hotel, Dallas, on his way to the airport."

Dallas's head jerked up. "To the airport?"

"Yes. Didn't Jane tell you? You're returning to Lexandros tomorrow."

"*No!*" Dallas stared at Jane. "She didn't say anything."

"Never mind. It's not important," he murmured lazily.

Dallas stood up, clenching her fists. "Oh,

but I think it is," she said quickly. "I mean, I don't quite know what your plans might be, but so far as I'm concerned, any return to the island would just be to collect our things before we leave!"

Alexander studied her pale cheeks with some deliberation. "You are not leaving," he said coldly. "That is understood."

"By whom?"

"By me, for one," exclaimed Jane.

Dallas gave her a hurt look. "Mr. Stavros," she began, "we're both very grateful to you for everything you've done for us, but it's over now. There's no more need for your protection. It was a period in time, that's all. And the period is over now."

Alexander's eyes were glacier-cold. "I disagree," he replied. "Does it not occur to you that Jane might require some time to recuperate from such a shattering experience?"

Dallas flushed. "Jane can recuperate in England. After all, it's early summer now. Even England has some good weather!"

"Stop being so damned awkward!" he muttered angrily, and then, as though remembering they had an audience, he said: "We'll sort this out, Jane. You just concentrate on getting well, again, hmm?" He walked to the door. "I will see you tomorrow, as arranged. Come, Dallas!"

Dallas wanted to refuse. She wanted to get as far away from him as she could, but without appearing childish she could only wish her sister goodbye for the present, and leave the room with as much dignity as she could muster.

Once outside the hospital, Dallas made to walk to where Stephanos was waiting for her with the car, but Alexander caught her arm in a hard, unyielding grip, and said:

"Come, I want to talk to you."

Dallas looked up at him, trying not to feel so emotional. "Anything you have to say, you can say right here."

He looked as though he was going to protest, to make her go with him by force, but then he changed his mind, and said:

"Very well, if you insist on behaving like the outraged sister!"

Dallas twisted her hands together. "What have you to say?" she asked in a tight little voice.

"Simply this—there will be no more talk of returning to England for the present time, is this understood?"

When Dallas did not reply, he went on:

"Just what do you imagine you will do when you return there? Your flat, I understand, is leased until the end of the summer. To whom do you intend going? Charles Jennings, perhaps?"

"My plans are no concern of yours," she retorted rudely.

"Oh, but they are," he said furiously. "Dallas, stop behaving so foolishly. I want you to go back to the island."

"Well, I don't want to go," she said tightly. "Besides, why do you want us to go back?"

"I do not intend to go into my reasons here, in the centre of one of Athens' main thoroughfares," he ground out angrily. "So! You will do as you are directed, and I will see you tomorrow afternoon when you arrive, with Jane. I myself am returning today. I have certain matters to attend to."

Dallas did not answer him, and with a muffled exclamation he turned and strode way down the sunlit street. Dallas watched him go with a feeling of despair.

Then she turned back to Stephanos, who had slid out of the car and come to join her. He nodded towards his employer's retreating figure.

"Do you do it on purpose?"

Dallas stared at him. "What?"

"Make him good and mad? Lord," he turned away, "I've never seen any woman treat Alex as you do. You ought to be careful. You're playing with dynamite!"

Dallas shook her head. "Oh, Stephanos," she said wearily, "I wish I knew what to do."

Stephanos gave her a strange look. "I guess you might remember that subordination does not come easily to Alex," he remarked enigmatically.

*　　*　　*

Dallas did not go to see Jane again that day. She could not bear the thought of the argument that would be bound to ensue. Jane wanted to go her way, as usual, and she would not contemplate any suggestion of Dallas's.

For Dallas the situation was intolerable. It was bad enough living on the island when their presence there was justified. Now it would seem like nothing but charity, and this was one thing she could not accept from Alexander Stavros. Maybe, if she had not cared for him, she would have been able to equate the situation with the upheaval in their two lives, and accept what the gods offered, as Jane was so fond of saying. But feeling as she did, going back there now would be too torturous. Living there, seeing him with Helen Neroulos, watching Madame Stavros manipulate them into the marriage she had desired for so long, would be more than she could bear.

As she lay on her bed in the early evening of that day, Dallas found her thoughts turning in another direction. Towards England, and Charles. She had no illusions about her feelings for Charles now, but she felt that if she were really desperate he would not let her down. It was true what Stavros had said, about their return to England. They had no immediate home, but if she had a base, at Charles's for example, she might be able to make other arrangements, temporarily.

Compared to the whiplash of Madame Stavros's cold opinions, Mrs. Jennings seemed barely uncongenial, and to be back among normal things, and normal surroundings, seemed all that she could hope for to retain her self-respect. If she were to return to Lexandros, and Alexander Stavros created another situation like the night at the cabin, she was afraid of her emotions destroying her completely.

With sudden decision, she slid off the bed, and reached for the telephone. She asked for the number of the international airport office, and once through, she asked whether there were any available seats on flights to London. As she waited for the girl to investigate, she thanked her stars that she had brought her handbag with her, and in it her passport and money. She had little of the latter, but once she arrived back in England, she could draw on their small savings until she resumed working. At least teaching positions were not too hard to find.

The airport receptionist was polite and thorough. There was a seat available on the seven a.m. flight to Gatwick the following morning. Dallas said she would take it. She gave her name, and the address of the hotel, half smiling when she reflected that from her address everyone would imagine she was rich and affluent. Still, she thought bleakly, her clothes would soon destroy that illusion, unless they considered her an eccentric millionairess.

She packed her suitcase with everything except the yellow two-piece she was wearing, phoned the reception desk and advised them that she would need a cab very early in the morning, and then sat down in a low arm-chair near the window to wait. She would not go to bed. There was no point really. She would never sleep, and besides, if she did drop off from complete exhaustion, she might miss her flight.

She watched the lights flicker out all over the city, and shivered a little before lighting another cigarette. There was no time so depressing or unnerving as those early hours before dawn.

She had never felt so alone in her life before. Even when her mother abandoned them, and her father was so broken up about it, she had still felt they had something, the three of them together. But now her father was dead, and Jane—well, she had realised that Jane was ultimately more capable of taking care of herself than she was. Maybe if she were more like Jane, things wouldn't hurt her so badly.

She stubbed out her cigarette and glanced at her watch. It was slowly passing, this terrible night of gloom. She stood up, stretched, and thrust the packet of cigarettes into her handbag. Then when the faint fingers of light were flooding the city with that magical dawn glow, she opened the door of her room—and came face to face with Alexander Stavros.

She stepped back, horrified, hardly able to believe her eyes.

"Hello, Dallas," he said, straightening up from his position against the wall opposite her door. He flexed his muscles tiredly, as though he had been standing there for some considerable time, and she bit her lips hard and said:

"Why are you here? I . . . I thought you were returning to Lexandros yesterday."

"So I did," he remarked evenly. "But I came back last night."

"Why?"

"Isn't that obvious?" he asked wearily. "Oh, come on, let's not stand at your door arguing. The other guests are still asleep. Go back into your room. I want to talk to you."

Dallas was too bemused to protest, and she stepped backwards into the room jerkily, and then standing her case on the floor, she walked to the wide windows and released the blinds, flooding the room with a golden, early morning glow.

Alexander Stavros shut the door, and leaned back against it. He was still wearing the same light blue suit he had been wearing the previous day, and there was a growth of beard on his face since he had not shaved that morning.

Dallas stood, her fingers linked tightly together, and he sighed heavily as he looked at her.

"Why do you do these things to me?" he murmured, shaking his head. "It's as well that I can read your mind. If I hadn't rung the airport last night and discovered what I had suspected might occur to you, you'd be hurrying off to take a plane, hundreds of miles away from me."

Dallas turned away. "It shouldn't matter to you what I do. Jane is your responsibility, not me. And she's perfectly capable of staying on the island, alone, until she decides she wants to come home."

"And where is home?" he asked softly. "I always thought that home was where the heart is."

Dallas bent her head. "Mr. Stavros, this conversation is getting us nowhere. Please let me go. I'll . . . I'll miss my plane."

He shrugged. "You will, anyway. I cancelled your booking last night."

She swung round to face him. "You did what!"

"I cancelled your booking. You won't be needing it."

Dallas stared at him. "Oh! *Oh!* Why can't you let me *go?* Jane doesn't need me!"

"No," he agreed quietly. "But *I* do."

Dallas turned cold, and then hot, and then trembled a little. "Now . . . now you're making fun of me," she said shakily.

"I can assure you," he said, with some irony, "it is not funny! For me, at least."

She could not look at him. "Please . . . " she began, shaking her head, while her mind and emotions churned uncontrollably.

"No, you please—*me*," he murmured, and straightening, he at last crossed the room towards her.

He lifted her chin with his fingers, looking down searchingly into her face. "I love you, Dallas," he said, in a low tone, that turned her knees to water. "And I've never said that to *any* woman before."

She still could not take it in, "Alexander!" she protested, turning her face away, and with increasing awareness of the nearness of her slender body, he slid his arms round her back, pressing her close against him.

"Oh, but I do," he murmured, caressing the side of her neck with his lips. "And I am

288

holding myself in check at this moment because after the night I have spent, waiting for you to really go through with leaving me, I ought to make love to you so violently that you just wouldn't have the strength to do that to me again." He buried his face in her hair, and she could feel him trembling. "You've got to marry me, Dallas. I can't live without you now."

"Oh, Alexander!" she breathed, two glistening tears sliding unheeded down her cheeks, as she turned her mouth to his.

At last he put her away from him, holding her at arm's length, his fingers hard upon her shoulders.

"I've wanted you for a long time," he murmured. "But every time I touched you I despised myself for taking advantage of your helpless situation. But I can't wait any longer. I need you more than my self-respect."

She stared at him tremulously. "You know I love you," she said helplessly. "But what about Helen?"

"Helen?" He frowned. Then he lifted his shoulders slightly. "I never wanted Helen, not even when I was engaged to her. If I had loved her I wouldn't have waited ten years to tell her so." He smiled gently. "I gather you've heard the story of my marriage."

She nodded. "Paula told me."

"I'm glad. You'll know I mean what I say when I tell you I love you."

Dallas couldn't believe it. It was too marvellous to be true. "What . . . what about your mother?" she asked quietly. "She wanted you to marry Helen."

He shrugged. "My mother and I have had a talk. I think we understand one another now. She's not such an ogre." He smiled. "Besides, as long as I am happy, she will be content." He chuckled. "Does that sound smug? It wasn't meant to."

"Oh, Alex," she whispered achingly. There was nothing more to say. "I'm so glad you came."

There was a sharp tap at the door. Alexander released her reluctantly, and went to open the door. The bellboy who stood there stared at him in amazement. "Mr. Stavros!" he exclaimed.

Alexander smiled at his confusion. "What is it you want?"

"I . . . the cab, for Miss Collins, is waiting. . . ."

"Cancel it," said Alexander easily. "She

won't be needing it now. Do you keep coffee in this hotel?"

The bellboy looked indignant. "Of every kind," he said.

"Then bring us some," Alexander nodded, then closed the door and leaned back against it, just looking at Dallas. Then he smiled, and said: "Where would you like to go for our honeymoon?"

THE END

ROMANCE TITLES IN THE ULVERSCROFT LARGE PRINT SERIES

Hospital Circles	*Lucilla Andrews*
A Hospital Summer	*Lucilla Andrews*
My Friend the Professor	*Lucilla Andrews*
The First Year	*Lucilla Andrews*
The Healing Time	*Lucilla Andrews*
Edinburgh Excursion	*Lucilla Andrews*
Highland Interlude	*Lucilla Andrews*
The Quiet Wards	*Lucilla Andrews*
Carpet of Dreams	*Susan Barrie*
The House of Conflict	*Iris Bromige*
Gay Intruder	*Iris Bromige*
Be My Guest	*Elizabeth Cadell*
The Haymaker	*Elizabeth Cadell*
The Past Tense of Love	*Elizabeth Cadell*
The Bespoken Mile	*March Cost*
The Hour Awaits	*March Cost*
Island of Mermaids	*Iris Danbury*
Penny Plain	*O. Douglas*
The Post at Gundooee	*Amanda Doyle*
My Friend Flora	*Jane Duncan*
Journey from Yesterday	*Suzanne Ebel*
The Half-Enchanted	*Suzanne Ebel*
The Doctor's Circle	*Eleanor Farnes*
The Constant Heart	*Eleanor Farnes*

Enchantment	*Mary Ann Gibbs*
The Scent of Water	*Elizabeth Goudge*
The Herb of Grace	*Elizabeth Goudge*
The Middle Window	*Elizabeth Goudge*
The Bird in the Tree	*Elizabeth Goudge*
The Heart of the Family	*Elizabeth Goudge*
The Castle on the Hill	*Elizabeth Goudge*
Doctor in Exile	*Maysie Greig*
Watch the Wall, My Darling	
	Jane Aiken Hodge
Sew a Fine Seam	*Mary Howard*
A Lady fell in Love	*Mary Howard*
Lovers all Untrue	*Norah Lofts*
Light from One Star	*Netta Muskett*
The Loom of Tancred	*Diane Pearson*
Wintersbride	*Sara Seale*
In Trust to Fiona	*Renée Shann*
Anna and her Daughters	*D. E. Stevenson*
Charlotte Fairlie	*D. E. Stevenson*
Katherine Wentworth	*D. E. Stevenson*
Celia's House	*D. E. Stevenson*
Winter and Rough Weather	
	D. E. Stevenson
Listening Valley	*D. E. Stevenson*
Bel Lamington	*D. E. Stevenson*
Fletcher's End	*D. E. Stevenson*
Spring Magic	*D. E. Stevenson*
The English Air	*D. E. Stevenson*

The House of the Deer	*D. E. Stevenson*
South to Forget	*Essie Summers*
The Lark in the Meadow	*Essie Summers*
The Bay of the Nightingales	*Essie Summers*
A Place Called Paradise	*Essie Summers*
Great House	*Kate Thompson*
Mandevilla	*Kate Thompson*
Sugarbird	*Kate Thompson*
Goddess of Threads	*Frances Turk*
The Man from Outback	*Lucy Walker*
The Man in Command	*Anne Weale*
The Silver Dolphin	*Anne Weale*
Love for Dr. Penn	*Kay Winchester*
Doctor Paul's Patient	*Kay Winchester*
The Goat Bag	*Susan Wingfield*
The Cazalet Bride	*Violet Winspear*
Tender is the Tyrant	*Violet Winspear*

THE WHITEOAK CHRONICLE SERIES TITLES IN THE ULVERSCROFT LARGE PRINT SERIES

by Mazo De La Roche

The Building of Jalna
Morning at Jalna
Mary Wakefield
Young Renny
Whiteoak Heritage
The Whiteoak Brothers
Jalna
Whiteoaks
Finch's Fortune
The Master of Jalna
Whiteoak Harvest
Wakefield's Course
Return to Jalna
Renny's Daughter
Variable Winds at Jalna
Centenary at Jalna

RELIGIOUS & DEVOTIONAL TITLES IN THE ULVERSCROFT LARGE PRINT SERIES

God Calling
My Utmost for his Highest
The Ulverscroft Large Print Hymn Book
Fellowship Hymnal

◆

The Ulverscroft Large Print Song Book
(Singing for Pleasure)

We hope this Large Print edition gives you the pleasure and enjoyment we ourselves experienced in its publication.

There are now 1,000 titles available in this ULVERSCROFT Large Print Series. Ask to see a Selection at your nearest library.

The Publisher will be delighted to send you, free of charge, upon request a complete and up-to-date list of all titles available.

Ulverscroft Large Print Books Ltd.
The Green, Bradgate Road
Anstey, Leicester
England